Athens County
Library Services
Nelsonville, Ohio

SILENCE ON THE SHORES

D0887318

SILENCE ON THE SHORES

(*Le Silence des rives*)

LEÏLA SEBBAR

Translated and with an introduction

by MILDRED MORTIMER

UNIVERSITY OF NEBRASKA PRESS

LINCOLN AND LONDON

WITHDRAWN

Athens County
Library Services
Nelsonville, Ohio

Publication of this translation was assisted
by a grant from the French Ministry of Culture—
National Center for the Book.

Le Silence des rives © 1993 Éditions Stock
Translation and introduction
© 2000 by the University of Nebraska Press
All rights reserved
Manufactured in the United States of America

∞

Library of Congress Cataloging-in-Publication Data
Sebbar, Leïla. [Silence des rives, English]
Silence on the shores / Leïla Sebbar ;
translated and with an introduction
by Mildred Mortimer.   p. cm.
Includes bibliographical references.
ISBN 0-8032-4285-9 (cl. : alk. paper)—
ISBN 0-8032-9276-7 (pbk.: alk. paper)
I. Mortimer, Mildred P.   II. Title.
PQ2679.E244 S5713 2000   843'.914—dc21   00-028651

ᴎ

3 2000 00011 0916

INTRODUCTION

Mildred Mortimer

Leïla Sebbar occupies a unique position in francophone Maghrebian literature. The daughter of an Algerian father and a French mother, she writes about Maghrebian immigrant society in France, identifying herself as a *croisée*, a hybrid at the intersection of Occidental and Oriental cultures. This Franco-Algerian novelist, who spent her formative years in Algeria and her adult life in France, uses writing to re-create the world of marginalized immigrants in order to lessen her own personal sense of exile. In a collaborative text on exile, an exchange of letters with the Canadian writer Nancy Huston, she writes:

> I am there at the crossroads, serene at last, finally in my place; for I am a *croisée* seeking a connection; writing within a lineage, one that is always the same. It is tied to history, to memory, to identity, to tradition, and to transmission, by which I mean the

The introduction first appeared as "Exile and Memory in Sebbar's *Le Silence des rives*," in *Research in African Literatures* 30.3 (fall 1999): 125–34, published by Indiana University Press.

search for ascendants and descendants, seeking a place in the history of a family, a community, a people with regard to History and the universe. It is in fiction that I feel that I am a free subject (free of father, mother, clan, dogma) and strengthened by the burden of exile. Only there do I muster body and soul to span the two banks, both upstream and downstream. (Sebbar and Huston 138)

Writing to connect herself to past and future communities, seeking "ascendants and descendants," she situates herself and her protagonists within a Mediterranean geographical and cultural context. In this letter to Huston, Sebbar's indirect reference to the Mediterranean that spans both French and Algerian shores anticipates the title of her eighth novel, *Silence on the Shores* (1993), a text depicting a day in the life of an Algerian immigrant in France who, as death draws near, returns through memory to the other shore, the Algeria of his childhood. In this novel, as in her previous work, exile, the legacy of the French colonial venture, means physical displacement, the immigration to France of economically disadvantaged Maghrebians, and results in psychological dislocation, fractured Maghrebian identity due to cultural marginalization on foreign soil.

A cultural hybrid, Sebbar shares common ground with Edward Said, who, as a Palestinian American scholar and critic, is also positioned at the crossing between East and West. They share this cultural space and have similar perspectives on Orientalism, a concept both view as a projection of the Westerner's fantasy—the colonial myth of the Other. In his reflection on a life in exile, "The Mind of Winter," Said delves into the meaning of such an experience, the gains and losses to the individual. Reminding his readers that the canon of modern Western culture is in large measure the achievement of exiles, émigrés, refugees, he states that their successes are undermined by a great sense of loss.

[vi]

Said defines exile in terms of pain: "Exile is the unhealable rift forced between a human being and a native place, between the self and its true home" (49). He explains, however, that plurality of vision compensates, at least in part, for the psychological dislocation: "Most people are principally aware of one culture, one setting, one home; exiles are aware of at least two, and this plurality of vision gives rise to an awareness of simultaneous dimensions, an awareness that—to borrow a phrase from music—is contrapuntal" (Said 55). With the adaptation to a new environment, the exile finds new customs, activities, expressions that occur *against* the memory of the old. The new does not replace the old but results in contrapuntal juxtaposition. Although the exile lives in a world that is admittedly decentered and nomadic, she or he finds enrichment through a greater sense of potential—a new way of seeing, hearing, and experiencing his or her surroundings. For Said, the ability to distance oneself, to see "the entire world as a foreign land" (55), grants a new and welcomed perspective.

Can the Maghrebian diaspora achieve the "contrapuntal awareness" that, in Said's view, compensates for the sense of loss? The challenge to all generations of Maghrebians in France is to redefine cultural space so that the North African culture of origin and the European culture in which they find themselves located—but not rooted—do not clash. They must appropriate a new space that is in some way distinct from dominant Western culture but maintains important links with it. Since they live in a francophone secular state in which the Arabic language and Islam are marginalized, their task is not easy. If their solution is to accept some elements of both East and West, they must choose wisely. But is it possible to find the proper balance, or must they embrace the West and abandon the Maghreb if they are to remain in France? Finally, how does Algeria's undeclared war between the military government and Islamic fundamentalists, with massacres that have taken the lives of tens of thousands of Algerians in the past few years, affect the social, economic, and philosophical choices of today's Maghrebian immigrants? As Sebbar explores these and related issues in her writings, it is difficult for her or anyone else to predict how Maghrebian cultural identity will express itself in France in the future, particularly if the political struggle that plagues Algeria today continues into the next millennium.

Sebbar grapples with questions of immigrant cultural identity on two fronts, in terms of two generations. In earlier texts—*Fatima ou les Algériennes au square* (1981), *Parle mon fils, parle à ta mère* (1984), and her Shérazade trilogy, *Shérazade, 17 ans, brune, frisée, les yeux verts* (1982), *Les Carnets de Shérazade* (1985), and *Le Fou de Shérazade* (1991)—she focused on the experiences of young Beurs, children of Maghrebian immigrants living in France, the second and third generations of North Africans, for whom the Maghreb is often either a hazy memory or a place they have learned about secondhand through stories, photos, family visitors. In *Silence on the Shores*, Sebbar examines the experiences of a middle-aged male immigrant caught between conflicting spaces—Algeria and France—who finds solace only with "city nomads like himself."

Examining Sebbar's fictional world of immigrants, we find the novelist using the theme of immigration to challenge the very concept of the French cultural identity. As Françoise Lionnet points out, by challenging the notion of *francité*, Sebbar compels her readers to rethink the linguistic and ideological categories French and francophone ("Logiques" 113). The critic concludes that Sebbar, with texts that do not fit into neat cultural categories but engage in the process of breaking the boundaries between them, does in fact belong to both.

Revisiting the Shérazade trilogy, we discover that although Sebbar uses themes that place her within the ranks of francophone writers (dislocation, historical amnesia, the plight of women silenced by patriarchy, and revolt against social constraints), she does not limit her focus to the world of North African immigrants but depicts the wide range of marginal types and ethnicities that form contemporary French society. For example, Shérazade's *squatt* shelters a disparate group of runaways, including idealistic revolutionaries and drug addicts. The young Beure's travels in France allow her to explore affinities between Maghrebian immigrants and the rural poor of France. Her extensive reading results in the discovery of literary figures such as Flora Tristan, Rimbaud, and Isabelle Eberhardt who, in their rebellion against French bourgeois society, chose exile and nomadism, leaving a textual legacy that Shérazade uses in the postcolonial present. Hence, in the trilogy, the young Beure explores texts, Orientalist painting, oral history, and popular culture to find the clues that will help her understand her position as a postcolonial nomad.[1] Thus, Sebbar's texts present a new France that Lionnet characterizes as a nation "tailored to the migrants working their way across it" (*Postcolonial* 177). Supporting Lionnet's analysis, Anne Donadey finds that Sebbar's writing redefines *francité* as "*métissage*, a term inclusive of people of Maghrebian descent" (270).

Depicting the final day in the life of a Maghrebian immigrant in France, *Silence on the Shores* explores the present world and past memories of a man whose life reveals shattered dreams and broken promises. Having crossed the Mediterranean as a young man to work in France, married a French woman, and remained on "the other shore," he broke the promise made to his mother to return home. Aware that death is drawing near, he fears experiencing the ultimate form of exile, dying alone, with no fellow Muslim at his side to whisper the traditional prayer to him in his final hours.

In this text, Sebbar's minimalist style conveys the simplicity of

1. For further studies of the Shérazade trilogy, see Mortimer (*Journeys*; "On the Road") and Woodhull.

everyday life on both shores of the Mediterranean—southern France where he lives, Algeria that he remembers. Through a series of monologues linked by associative memory, the narrative foregrounds the fragmentation and sense of discontinuity experienced by the immigrant in his daily life as it uncovers the varied facets of exile and the role of memory in easing the pain. The reader accompanies the man on his interior and exterior journeys, moving from interior monologue to free indirect discourse and back, traveling through time and space with the protagonist, who spends the first day of summer—his last—on "the other shore."

In *Silence on the Shores*, Sebbar's characters are nameless. Just as the protagonist is called "the man," other characters in turn are termed "the child," "the mother," "the three sisters." Not only does anonymity add a mysterious and timeless quality to the narrative, it transforms an individual's story into a parable of exile and errancy. Anonymous in exile, the man has neither a first name that would give him individuality nor a last name that would attach him to a lineage; with no specific identity, he is, in fact, Everyman. In this respect, he is very different from Shérazade of Sebbar's trilogy, named for the legendary storyteller of *The Arabian Nights* and thereby placed at the center of texts that challenge the discourse of European Orientalism.

As the novel opens, announcing the impending death of the protagonist on the first page ("At the bend in the river, he fell"), the theme of death is omnipresent. Death, the grim reaper, will strike in a variety of ways: a child is killed by a blow from a horse's hooves; a family perishes in a cholera epidemic; a woman dies in childbirth; a young Beur is shot by a neighbor; a roofer falls to his death; a family dies in an earthquake. These sudden, violent, and unexpected deaths woven through the text contrast with the natural death of the aged matriarch. Announced at the beginning of the novel, the latter had occurred on the first day of summer many years earlier in a room overlooking a Moorish courtyard with a flowing fountain. The flowing fountain marks Edenic time, the era before men began to leave the seaside village in search of work on the other shore, before the "big house" left unattended had fallen into disrepair, and before the fountain had dried up.[2]

For the matriarch's granddaughter (the man's mother), however, the peaceful passing of the old woman on that first day of summer is disrupted by the arrival of the three sisters, washers of the dead, who seem to know intuitively when and where death hovers. The man recalls in detail his mother's description of the event as her words first evoked for him the visual image of the trio that had come to prepare her grandmother's funeral: "The vagabond sisters roam barefoot, cloaked in torn veils, their heads covered with black headscarves— even if they are not black, she sees them as black as pieces of old fabric people throw on garbage heaps far from the village; the sisters are seated in the room around the low table." Seen through a child's eyes, the three sisters appear as sinister, unkempt vagabonds, strangers to be feared.

Who are these mysterious figures inextricably linked to death and mourning? They suggest the three sisters of the underworld of Greek and Roman mythology as well as the witches of *Macbeth*. Feared by the villagers because of their seemingly mysterious powers, forbidding appearance, incomprehensible language, and nomadic existence, they are the excluded. As witches, they are feared; as washers of the dead, they are needed. Women who appear to have no fixed home, who roam the countryside, and who live from time to time in the Roman ruins at the edge of the village, they represent marginality within the Algerian rural context. They are, therefore, the reverse

2. In Arab countries, the courtyard with the center fountain is meant to suggest the image of terrestrial paradise. See Chevalier and Gheerbrant (453–54).

image of the marginalized Other in France, where various groups and individuals are excluded because of dress, customs, and language and feared because of their difference. In a text in which there is easy slippage from one monologue to another, the mother's narrative gives way to voices of women in the *hammam* (the Moorish bath), who, in an attempt to shed light on the mysterious strangers, move into imaginative space, projecting their own fantasies upon them, thereby creating within their own context a myth of the Other.[3]

As Shérazade sought clues to help her understand her position as a postcolonial nomad, the man, a contemporary of her father's generation, embarks upon a similar identity quest. He uses orality in his quest, listening attentively to the female voices of his past to come to grips with the meaning of life as an exile. Although, as Said reminds us, exile is fundamentally a discontinuous state of being (the individual separated from his or her homeland and past), Sebbar's protagonist is able to retrieve the past through memory despite geographical separation. In effect, what he does not secure in space—the physical return to Algeria—he constructs in time, returning through memory.

The memory of the matriarch's death, concomitant with the three sisters' appearance, initiates an introspective journey that reveals oppositions between mother and son originating in the difference in the worldview between migrating men and sedentary women. This spatial division between men and women that exists in the Maghreb finds expression in the Berber proverb "Man is the outer lamp; woman is the inner lamp." Men inhabit public space, women private space; men travel abroad, women stay at home.

3. He learns later that the community opinion has become more realistic with regard to the sisters: "The sisters who are not really sisters are poor harmless women, slightly crazy. They are neither magicians nor priestesses, nor witches of any kind, but vagabonds who do honorable but degrading work."

Village women waiting patiently for their men to come home learn that most men appear to lose their way. In this family, the oldest son, by marrying and settling in France, breaks his promise to return; the youngest son, killed in an accident, comes home in a coffin. Hence, despite their fidelity, women often find themselves abandoned. Moreover, the men who do come home do not stay long. Upon their return, they are eager to sleep with their wives but neglect the household repairs the women require of them.

Most importantly, however, the pattern of male migration results in both women's increased sense of domesticity and men's transiency. This gender division finds expression in the distinctly different attitudes toward two related issues: attachment to the family home (and, therefore, the land) and burial. Although the mother is intent upon keeping the house from falling into decay, the son is not. He would not listen "when his cousin talked about the house that needed repairing, and the fountain that wasn't working, and the pillars about to collapse. He said no, he wouldn't come home."

Attached to her home in life and in death, the mother gives explicit instructions to her family regarding her burial in the village cemetery. Her son, in contrast, expresses his desire to be buried at sea. Thus, in death as in life, she affirms rootedness, he expresses errancy. The son's final wish, however, remains ambiguous. His instruction that his body be sent out to sea, "where the river and sea come together," may be interpreted as his wish to return home, to recross the Mediterranean, at least symbolically, or it may signify his intent to disappear into liminal space, the realm between the two shores, where he may be lost to both.

Rooted to the land, unable to embark upon adventures that would carry them beyond domestic space, the women remaining at home do find their lives circumscribed. Although the blond, curly-haired cousin played freely in the Roman ruins as a little girl, at puberty her movements were restricted. Moreover, she and the other women dwell in a landscape of decay and ruins. The seaside village is bordered by Roman ruins, the place the three sisters inhabit when they come to town. In addition to these ancient ruins, the women encounter newer examples of decay: the dilapidated houses that provoke the mother's warning. She is convinced that the crumbling pillars, whose deterioration she attributes to itinerant men's negligence, put them all at risk: "they would die under the debris caused not by an earthquake but because the men had forgotten the house."

As Serge Ménager notes, all the women live among the ruins, those who bring forth life and those who tend to the dead (61). Elaborating upon the link between the women and their decaying homes, the critic views the women as both the victims and the guardians of a nation whose decaying architectural constructions are symbolic of general decay: "Algeria has become nothing more than a communal grave for the large number of cadavers that appear throughout Sebbar's text and define the country as a cemetery" (Ménager 60).

To what extent do the decaying houses represent Algeria? It seems that Sebbar is showing that emigration, the departure of manpower from Algerian villages to metropolitan France, has sapped Algeria's economic power and energy as it continues to pull at the cultural fabric of the nation as well. With no temporal references except the cyclical return to the first day of summer (the day of the matriarch's demise and the man's impending death), it is difficult for the reader to establish a time frame for either the man's childhood in Algeria or his adult life in France, but it is most likely that he immigrated to France during the mid- to late 1960s. Sebbar suggests this possibility when, toward the end of the text, he meets a Maghrebian immigrant like himself who has just lost his childhood companion: "He talked about a childhood friend. They had gone to school together, and in the summer they watched their flocks in the mountains. They parted when the war broke out and met up again in the same resistance group. One of them almost died in the resistance, and the other spent time in prison, where his friend helped him until *their country was liberated, but they didn't remain there.*" If they immigrated following Algerian independence in 1962, these men represent the many young Algerians who, instead of participating in the development of the newly independent nation for which they had fought, slipped into a form of neocolonial dependency, earning paychecks in France to support their families at home. Although Sebbar portrays a worker who arrives alone and unattached in France, the pattern of immigration has changed considerably since the 1960s, with increasing numbers of workers bringing their families as well as a steady increase in the number of children born in France of Maghrebian immigrants (Hargreaves 8–12).

The man reveals that while in France he married a French woman. The marriage turned out badly, but they have not separated. Strangers to one another, they still share a house, but with no intimacy in the marriage, this house is not a home. Neither a refuge nor a center for shared values, the house and the rooms within it reinforce the protagonist's sense of exile. Gaston Bachelard's analysis of intimate space, *The Poetics of Space*, posits home as the crucial site of one's intimate life, the refuge where memory and imagination serve to integrate life experiences. The phenomenologist uses the term *espace heureux* (felicitous space) to designate his concept of intimate space, the anchor without which men and women become fragmented individuals. Deprived of intimate space, the man is denied the nurturing space that would allow him to feel at home on "the other shore."

In his topoanalysis (the study of the sites of intimate life), Bachelard traces men's and women's experiences of interior and exterior space to childhood. He explains that our impressions of subjective and objective reality are formed first in childhood, then transformed by present reality and projected upon a future. In the present, we tend to remember our childhood home with nostalgia as we project onto the future an image of our ideal home.[4] The man's experiences of subjective and objective reality, like those of every uprooted individual, have been formed in a childhood home situated elsewhere. As images filter through the pane of memory, his childhood home, the rambling Moorish-style house situated in a village on the Algerian coast, emerges as a refuge, but only as a referent to the past. For this immigrant, home exists in the realm of the imaginary but not the real. Thus, in daily life, he encounters the "unhomely," which Homi Bhabha defines as "the estranging sense of the relocation of the home and the world in an unhallowed place" (141), the sentiment of alienation experienced by fellow uprooted marginalized individuals, inhabitants of bidonvilles (African shantytowns) and cités (housing projects on the outskirts of major French cities).

Sebbar's protagonist understandably finds his refuge in public space—cafés frequented by other Maghrebian workers—and in nature—quiet fishing spots along the river that flows into the sea. Relationships in the cafés, however, remain distant; he rarely sees the same faces more than once and does not ask their names. Yet it is here that he finds the comfort of imaginative creative space. A poet, he often writes at a café table and, reading his poems aloud, shares his creative work with his fellow immigrant workers. In this way, he mirrors the creative process that in part characterizes the novelist's own work habits. As Sebbar explains in her exchange of letters with Huston, she writes in cafés and brasseries, often using "a piece of the paper tablecloth, sugar cube wrappers, the back of a bill" (Sebbar and

---

4. Bachelard writes: "When we dream of the house we were born in, in the utmost depths of revery, we participate in this original warmth, in this well-tempered matter of the material paradise" (7).

Huston 9) on which to note her thoughts. Thus, as Sebbar jots down ideas and impressions in Parisian cafés, her protagonist covers sheets of paper with his poems in a similar space. Both have found an alternative or third space, one that is public yet private, friendly yet anonymous. It is fluid space that one may enter with a specific purpose—a meeting, a task, an agenda—or leave open to chance and unexpected encounters.

If Maghrebian café companions support the man's creativity and are receptive to his work, his French wife is not. She wishes him to enter her world but will not approach his. Refusing to return to Algeria with her husband, she also refuses to acknowledge his creativity or take part in it. After forgetting to put away the pages of a story he had written, he discovers that she has destroyed his work, burning his papers in the fireplace. Censoring his writing, she effectively silences him; he is unable either to reconstruct the story or articulate his hurt and anger at the destruction of his work.

Uprooted, decentered, living on the margins of a European culture that does not value his own, Sebbar's protagonist is representative of the immigrant caught between two worlds, a homeland in decay and a host country where she or he faces erasure, silencing, and invisibility. Exiled from her own place of origin, Sebbar uses writing, as Donadey asserts, as a locus for reterritorialization (270). Struggling to secure her place in the world through the creative act of writing, the Franco-Algerian writer is committed to giving Maghrebian immigrants a legitimate space in French literature. Yet her texts reveal how difficult it is for the minority voice to be heard as long as the dominant hegemonic discourse continues to resist.

As he feels death drawing near, Sebbar's protagonist strips himself of his poetry. He tosses his writing into the water where the river joins the sea. After scattering his poems in the river, he imagines them being carried by swallows across the sea, reaching the seaside

[xvii]

village where the youngest of the three sisters will reassemble the fragments and slip them under the door of his mother's house. Through pure magic realism, the sea transports his poetry home, carrying his words back to maternal space. At the end of his life, the Mediterranean no longer separates him from his origins but reconnects the links of communication disrupted by a broken promise. We readers never read the man's poetry (just as we never get to peek into Shérazade's notebooks). Hence, we must accept on faith the premise that the poems express his sensibility and are, like Sebbar's own literary work, "strengthened by the burden of exile."

Having feared silence, solitude, and the absence of the traditional prayer, the man is consoled in his final hours by the presence of a companion, a man like himself who whispers into his ear the prayer for the dead. Having feared the absence of this ritual on the foreign shore, he is granted the prayer. And as he listens to a fraternal voice expressing these comforting words in his maternal language, his long years of exile draw to a close.

In conclusion, this errant life that ends on the first day of summer has been marked by "the mind of winter," a term Said borrows from the American poet Wallace Stevens, using it to situate exile in a space where "the pathos of summer and autumn as much as the potential of spring are nearby but unobtainable" (55). As Sebbar has shown, the exile's life is decentered, insecure, and painful at times, but a life spent outside habitual order often leads to originality of vision, the "contrapuntal awareness" that inspires and accomplishes significant creative work such as her own.

WORKS CITED

Bachelard, Gaston. *The Poetics of Space*. Trans. Marie Jolas. Boston: Beacon Press, 1994.

Bhabha, Homi. "The World and the Home." *Social Text* 31 / 32, 10.2–3 (1992):141–53.

Chevalier, Jean, and Alain Gheerbrant. *Dictionnaire des symboles*. Paris: Robert Laffont / Jupiter, 1982.

Donadey, Anne. "Cultural Métissage and the Place of Identity in Leïla Sebbar's Shéra-zade Trilogy." *Borders, Exiles, Diaspora*. Ed. Elazar Barkan and Marie-Denise Shelton. Stanford CA: Stanford University Press, 1998. 257–73.

Hargreaves, Alec. "Ni Beurs, ni immigrés, ni jeunes issus de l'immigration." *Bulletin of Francophone Africa* 11 (1997): 8–12.

Lionnet, Françoise. " 'Logiques métisses': Cultural Appropriation and Postcolonial Representations." *College Literature* 19.3 (October 1992) and 20.1 (February 1993):102–20.

——. *Postcolonial Representations: Women, Literature, Identity*. Ithaca NY: Cornell University Press, 1995.

Ménager, Serge D. "Sur la forme du roman de Leïla Sebbar *Le silence des rives*." *Etudes Francophones* 12.2 (1997):55–65.

Mortimer, Mildred. *Journeys through the French African Novel*. Portsmouth: Heinemann, 1990.

——. "On the Road: Leïla Sebbar's Fugitive Heroines." *Research in African Literatures* 23.2 (summer 1992):195–201.

Said, Edward. "The Mind of Winter." *Harper's Magazine* (September 1984):49–55.

Sebbar, Leïla. *Fatima ou les Algériennes au square*. Paris: Stock, 1981.

——. *Shérazade, 17 ans, brune, frisée, les yeux verts*. Paris: Stock, 1982.

——. *Parle mon fils, parle à ta mère*. Paris: Stock, 1984.

——. *Les Carnets de Shérazade*. Paris: Stock, 1985.

——. *Le Fou de Shérazade*. Paris: Stock, 1991.

——. *Le Silence des rives*. Paris: Stock, 1993.

Sebbar, Leïla, and Nancy Huston. *Lettres parisiennes*. Paris: Bernard Barrault, 1986.

Woodhull, Winifred. *Transfigurations of the Maghreb: Feminism, Decolonization, and Literatures*. Minneapolis: University of Minnesota Press, 1993.

SILENCE ON THE SHORES

I

At the bend in the river, he fell.

Who will come to the other bank, to the white room where for so
many days I have been alone, and whisper in my ear the prayer for the
dead?
Who will speak my mother's words to me?

I

Who will be able to speak to me, when I am so far away from her? I
don't know she is already buried near the little sanctuary of dried
stones in the maritime cemetery, in the shade, next to her mother's
tomb, where her mother's mother was laid to rest.

On washdays, sitting on her straw mat in front of a laundry basin,
leaning against the pillar that is cracked in several places, his mother
used to tell the women of the family, laughing through her tears, that
one day they would be crushed by the pillars that were too fragile to
support an abandoned house any longer. Everything is old; no one

takes care of the house the women inhabit and repaint with white-wash and a blue trim at the base of the wall in order to hide the crumbling surface. Did his mother listen to what was said by her sisters-in-law, as well as by the neighbors, some young, some old, all carefree and unaware they would die under the debris caused not by an earthquake but because the men had forgotten the house? They thought only of their wife's body, at night, when they arrived secretly, but she would awaken from the deepest sleep at the sound of bare feet moving furtively across the tile floor and up to the high bed. She knew, she . . . his mother . . . And her predictions, which the women began to fear as the first cracks appeared in the pillars, foreshadowed not only their death under the stones and the roof tiles but her own death, and what she wanted to be done. But who would do it? What if, at that moment, not one woman listened to her; what if not one were to offer serene supportive gestures, so that she would be buried according to custom, wrapped in the shroud she had kept hidden in her bride's trousseau. She had purchased it in secret from the dry goods salesman to whom she had given the measurements; he had prepared the most beautiful piece of fabric, the whitest woven bleached flax, which he wrapped in thick rough butcher's paper that was gray with black or dark blue specks. At the bottom of the trunk, in a fine wool blanket woven by her mother, she hid the shroud between two table settings, beside the linen, under the square piece of cloth she and her sisters had woven for their wedding night. Which one of them soiled the virgin's handkerchief with the blood of a chicken, a pigeon, or a dove, birds from the courtyard or their grandmother's coop? Not she. She had followed the rules, waiting for the day and the hour of the night when she would be loved by the man who had been chosen for her and whom she didn't love. For the tasks of watching over her, washing her, removing all her body hair, perfuming her, dressing her and wrapping her in the beautiful white sheet, reciting the prayers, and supervising the old women, those impious vagabonds who try to collect the water used to wash a body placed on the stone before being lifted onto the wooden stretcher, for these tasks his mother insists repeatedly that she wants a young girl. And if she is not a virgin, she must be a woman who has remained chaste for several days, as is customary during the month of Ramadhan, and that if such a woman exists, she must stay with her in her final hours and remain afterward, right up until the burial. She must not cry, she must speak to her in the language of her childhood, reciting poems learned from books, choosing the most beautiful verses to recite as if she were singing, and she must do this after making the women leave, all of them, including her sisters who are still alive. Her mother, who has already died, is waiting for her at the foot of the marabout's tomb, on the hill overlooking the sea in the maritime cemetery; she knows the exact spot. No woman should remain, not even those who wash the dead; they must be chased away despite their witches' cries; she doesn't want them there. She has told this to her oldest son, the one who now walks along the river, on the other side of the sea. She is waiting for him to return. He disappeared one morning, she doesn't know where; she hasn't seen him since. She's still waiting for him to return.

2

The man walks along the river.

His mother told him, so often . . .

The three sisters were there for her mother's mother. She, a little girl at the time, was frightened by these old women who should have died long ago. These women of misfortune had settled into her grandmother's room, the one that opens onto the fountain where the water was still flowing, the largest, brightest, most beautiful room. She saw them arrive at the end of the street; she understood because the children fled from them without uttering a sound; they were afraid, they knew what these women wanted. There were three of them, inseparable, arriving on foot, one of them gripping an olive-wood cane. When her old aunt died, the oldest asked for this cane she had wanted for a long time. She was already limping, and they gave it to her, despite the objections of the aunt's children, because they feared she would curse the family, since she knew all the expressions and the rites that bring forth misfortune. She took the cane without a word and comes back each time; why doesn't she ever die . . . There are three of them; people say they are sisters, but who knows them? They come from far away, no one knows where their village is, they reveal nothing about themselves, not even their first names. They are called the sisters—when they arrive in the village, no one knows whose daughters they are. Do witches have mothers? Are they the daughters of a man and a woman? Without a family, without children, they are vagabonds who go from house to house, without ever getting it wrong; they go wherever a woman . . . a man . . . a child is dying. They know. When she was a little girl, she wondered if these women were mortal like the others, her aunt, her grandmother, or the old orphaned cousin the family had taken in to look after the house and the children. The sisters walk in step with the one who limps; she is the one in charge. The children run away, disappear behind the walls of the houses, spy on the sisters from behind open doorways, whisper, provide commentary for the women who come running over from the big house. The youngest women look on from the terrace where the others have left the spices and raisins they were sorting. The youngest sister carries a bundle slung on a stick, which she uses to shoo away the boldest children, and there are very few she does not intimidate. They are heard speaking as they go toward the house with the green front door, the one where the grandmother is dying. Who can understand what they are saying to each other? As if

[4]

they were speaking a foreign tongue, the women listen without being able to make any sense of their obscure words, words as black as the clothing they have been wearing for years. The black fabric, worn and dusty, has turned grayish green. No one goes to greet them. The women surrounding the dying woman wait in the courtyard near the fountain. The grandmother can still hear the water running; she is the one who kept asking for the fountain to be repaired, because of the sound of the water, and because she rinsed her figs under the clear spray before eating them at dawn. She is on her deathbed this first day of summer when the flowers on the fig trees are still green; but the water in the fountain flows for her as she lies in the open room. She is stretched out on the sofa; her mattress placed on the stone slab faces the fountain tiled with ancient blue and green tiles whose colors are barely visible. She does not hear the sisters' footsteps as they enter the house. They are no longer speaking, nor are the women waiting for them. The sisters bow before the oldest woman, who precedes them into the grandmother's room. The little girl follows the women she calls the witches, hiding in the folds of her mother's dress at the entrance to the room. The sisters have seated themselves at the foot of the bed where the old woman is moaning softly. They rock back and forth, reciting words that do not seem to be part of the language she hears and speaks in her grandmother's house. They recite for a long time, patiently, in a language that is not spoken here; it is the language of sacred verses, the tongue witches speak among themselves. What will happen to grandmother if the sisters do not say what must be said for her to find her place at God's right hand? The little girl thinks her grandmother will be the first, among women and men, to occupy the best place. As the sisters sit cross-legged at the end of the sofa, speaking with their eyes closed, do they know what they are saying? Are they saying what they should? Who can tell? Their language is secret. The women of the

house do not seem much concerned about what the sisters are reciting, the sisters who will come for them as well. The little girl watches
her mother, standing at the entrance of the room near her cousin; she
pulls at her dress to warn her, to tell her to be suspicious of the
foreign words that might harm her grandmother, but her mother lets
the women rock back and forth and repeat their strange litanies; the
mother puts her hand on the little girl's mouth; no one must speak,
the sisters know what they are doing, they have always done things
this way, they will continue until the end of time. And who will take
care of the last one of them, the one who will die after the other two,
who will do that? Her body will be left to the jackals in the hills, or
perhaps she will have met up with another sister, and she will walk
with her across fields and through villages, going from one corpse to
another, washing them with the appropriate words and gestures that
others do not know. Hearing the sound coming from the grandmother's mouth, the sisters know she has just died. They suddenly
cease their prayers, rise, and lean over the dead woman, three black
shadows that keep the little girl from seeing her grandmother. She
wanted to hold her hand, but she was moved away from her; she
wanted to speak to her but was told to keep quiet because of the
sisters who are now busy with the body she cannot see. Her mother
pushes her back roughly, ordering her to join the children in the
other courtyard as she in turn enters the funeral chamber with the
women. Cries and sobs are heard. The little girl recognizes the stri-
dent voice of the witches who, having no home of their own, travel
roads, woods, plateaus, and deserts, speaking to jackals and hyenas,
unearthing corpses in cemeteries at night, cutting off hands for their
diabolical potions, killing serpents and frogs, and bearing bad news
and the evil eye wherever they go. The women of the house let them
shout and cry; what will become of her grandmother surrounded by
these cursed lamentations, she who loved the sound of water, the

[6]

sound of the fountain? As the favorite grandchild, she would have recited the most beautiful verses of the sacred book for her while clasping her delicate brown hand. She can no longer hear the lamentations taken up by the other women and her mother; she escapes, not wanting to stay with the children in the courtyard behind the house. They are playing and laughing; no one is watching her, so she leaves the house and runs without stopping up to the hill that looks out over the sea. She does not enter the cemetery; later she will go with the women to fill the bird's watering bowl and place a fresh myrtle or olive branch on the grave. She will sit in the shade of the marabout's tomb, lean against her grandmother's tomb, and speak to her in secret. She stops under the tree at the bottom of the hill, a cypress she has often leaned against while weeping. She is alone there, the tree protecting her from the women's cries, and she sobs, sitting down, facing the sea. When she returns to the house, she knows she has already chosen her resting place next to the marabout's tomb of dried stones near her grandmother. And these black women, these witches, will be dead, they will be the last of the washers of the dead. For her, from that day on, she insists she wants none of them, she will chase them away; she will get up from her deathbed to forbid them to enter her room, the one that opens onto the fountain that has not yet run dry. It is summer. The first day of summer. It is warm at night. The little girl climbs up to the terrace where the mats and rugs are left; the children will sleep there with the two orphaned servants barely older than themselves. The vagabond sisters roam barefoot, cloaked in torn veils, their heads covered with black head-scarves—even if they are not black, she sees them as black as pieces of old fabric people throw on garbage heaps far from the village; the sisters are seated in the room around the low table. The women serve them; they have voracious appetites and ask for coffee all night long. They never sleep. The children on the terrace stay up late waiting for their mothers, but they will not come to see them this night or the next because they are attending to the needs of the three sisters, who are taking charge of the women's ceremonies. The sisters chant a long time before going to sleep at dawn, each one lying on a mat at the foot of the sofa where the grandmother rests, wrapped in her shroud, the same as the one for her daughter and her daughter's daughter.

3

The sisters took away some food in a small bundle carried on the end of a stick, their money hidden in a leather purse worn against their dry breast. The village streets are empty, neither dogs nor boys chase them; the cane of the limping sister can be heard, the sisters are not speaking. The children have deserted the Roman ruins by the sea; the sisters walk toward the arena and sit down in the shade of the columns. The city will be theirs for three full days, until the next death occurs beyond the hill where villagers are beginning to thresh wheat, and men can be heard herding their animals. One of the sisters turns her head toward the cries above—just faint sounds in the distance—when the youngest leans toward her elders to talk to them about the village they are climbing up to on dirt paths at dusk; they can see night falling . . . Children watch them from behind the branches of rosemary bushes surrounded by the sweet sound of bees. Fishermen who live not far from the ruins, which have not yet been fenced in, have built beehives, and their bees fly between the lavender and the rosemary. The sisters wait patiently, their faces turned toward the hill on the other side of the road. The sea air does not prevent them from breathing in the smell of the land. They stay there for a long time, in silence, until the moment when the oldest raises her finger as if to point to the place from which death will come next. The sisters murmur. Night falls. They have not risen. The children are no longer there. The peasants on the hill have stopped working, but

[8]

they remain on watch. The sisters throw away chicken bones and bread crumbs, shake out the folds of their dresses and veils, and walk on toward the sea. In single file, they go up to the first wave, lean over, and collect the foam in the palms of their hands to wet their faces. They are alone on the beach. Each one carries out her ablutions slowly and methodically. The night is dark, and the foam at their feet is luminous. On the cobblestones of the Roman road, the olive-wood cane marks the uneven steps of the oldest. They stop near an altar at a place protected by walls that are still standing. Taking a handkerchief from their bundle, a clean handkerchief given to them in the house of the old grandmother, whose fresh tomb has been covered with brambles to prevent its being desecrated by jackals, they offer a final prayer before beginning the arduous climb up to the threshing ground in front of the house of a dying person, a child or a woman. It is probably a small child, given the wails they heard in the afternoon; they never mistake the shouts of men at work for the sound of a mother's lamentation. They spoke among themselves, their ears tuned to the voice of sorrow, the oldest deciding (she is always right). She said that it was a child, the firstborn boy—he was not stillborn but was crushed by a horse's hoof while they were threshing the wheat; he was two years old. He should not have been with the men and the animals when the sun was at its peak. He had slipped away. Now his mother and the other women can only scream and cry. The child is dying, he will have passed on by the time they arrive at the house, using the paths traced between the wheat fields. The horses are unharnessed. When they pass through the valley, the horses rise and come up to them. The sisters are not afraid. It is said that when they were young they used to ride dressed as Arab riders, galloping across the high plateaus and riding up to desert towns, where they would trot alongside huge cemeteries in the sand before stopping to rest beside a marabout's shrine gleaming green and gold in the sunset. They pause under a giant olive tree, between two mounds, before the first houses. The horses are standing facing them as they pat their muzzles with small strokes. The animals follow them to the edge of the dirt path and stop at the threshing field in front of the house where the women are holding their vigil. The sisters enter the small courtyard that has no fountain. A woman opens the curtain in front of the door of the low room. The young mother comes toward them, kissing the right hand of each one, inviting them to enter the room where the child lies asleep on a rug, a rug fit for his size, a prayer rug that will cover the wooden stretcher the men will carry up to the cemetery at the foot of the hill, at the edge of the wheat fields.

4

These women, witches who didn't stop chanting in their language for days on end, the mother of the man who walks along the river does not want to see them when death comes for her in the house of her mother's mother and those who had come before her. The house is so old, the men leave to work far away, and they forget their women live there, with no protection, cracked walls and pillars, the terrace unsafe, and the fountain no longer working; even the fig tree is dying; it still produces figs, but every year people say this will be the last, but that isn't true. The tree is sturdy, sturdier than the house the men don't take the time to repair; they say they don't have the money; they cross the sea to earn it. They come back and think of nothing except having more and more babies. She said the women will all be crushed to death—mothers, daughters, wives, sisters, sisters-in-law, cousins, aunts—the men will find only shattered stone, and they, the women, underneath, decaying, and then they won't be able to bear them any more children. She laughs when she speaks like this, but the other women don't laugh; they mutter among themselves that their young sister may be mad. She doesn't know what she's saying; they should call a marabout or a sorceress. His mother doesn't listen to them and speaks only of the impending catastrophe that will occur because the men have abandoned them, and even though she doesn't love her husband, he must not leave her to die without a tomb. The women are afraid, but she is the strongest, the only one capable of predicting the future, of preventing it, of using whitewash and blue paint so as not to die of shame. She is the only one who dares speak of her death and who says what she wants and what she doesn't want when the time comes. The men are young, it's true, they won't die now; they will come back for their women and will make love to them in a room under a roof that will soon cave in, but if one of the men should die far away, across the sea—one of the fathers, husbands, sons, cousins, brothers, uncles—because they all leave, the sons as well . . . She knows they have no reason to go, but they do not want to stay, and who is going to stop them if even their beautiful adoring wives cannot keep them? Do the sons die over there? And if they grow old without seeing their wives, mothers, or houses again, if they say they will return in the summer, but they don't come back this summer or the next or the following one, then the years pass, a mother grows old, a mother dies too.

And the son, the man walking by the river, forgets. He is not aware that the sisters are on the prowl; they have been seen in the region. They are waiting to enter the village where the dilapidated old house is caving in. They will sing, wail, shriek, they won't stop until they die, if the men don't come back in time to fix up the house and embrace their women. Every wash day (why that particular day?) he would hear his mother's complaints as he sat pressed against her thigh in front of the basin filled with foaming white water.

At that time he still went to the baths with his mother and the women of the big house.

5

The three women left the village of the wheat fields after the child's burial, the men arguing over who would carry the body placed on the oversized stretcher for the short distance. Those who did would be purified, would become wiser. Neither the mother nor the women accompanied the funeral procession to the olive tree at the bottom of the hill; the women remained, standing, forming a crestlike barrier, but who was their enemy? But the sisters followed the men up to the very tiny tomb under the vine-covered tree, beyond the mounds and the last bundles of wheat; the women posted silently at the edge of the village heard the sisters' funeral dirges—it is said they compose poems for the dead; as for which one of them invents the verses they sing in praise of God, the Prophet, and the Saints, it seems it is the youngest sister. Who will ever know the truth? Respect for the dead forbids one from asking about family ties to any of the mysterious women who have appeared from nowhere, just at the right moment, and who know the right gestures, voice, songs to accompany those who have left this world and whom love would tearfully abandon to solitude were they not present. The sisters fear neither cold nor death, they touch lifeless bodies as if they were still alive, bodies cradled by the murmur of verses sung in God's language. The women, despite what people say, obey the sisters carrying out the rite they respect; they are the only ones to do it perfectly. Who taught them? What vagabond women seated in the sandy cemeteries at the foot of the oldest marabout's tomb, whose cupola is repainted white every year, took the time to speak to the new arrivals, explaining to them in language unknown to the uninitiated the sacred rites that protect the least forgotten and least solitary dead, the person who doesn't leave behind a sterile house, abandoned to the hyenas? People say that the youngest of the sisters—the women seem to sense which one she is without the proof of identity papers—is the one who composes funeral verses, elegies as beautiful as wedding songs, although the sisters are never invited to weddings; and when one disastrous day they were seen entering the main room of the Moorish bath, the women covered their bodies and took refuge by huddling against one another on the stone benches at the back of the alcoves, their faces hidden by the flaps of their bathrobes, acting as if the sisters had come to choose their next victims.

6

This is what the women in the baths told each other, not suspecting that one day, one of them in her old age and misfortune would join the two orphaned sisters of the oldest one, the one who limps. Speaking all at once as they always do, seated cross-legged on the stone benches, the youngest listening at their feet without interrupting them, they said that one of the sisters, the sisters who attend to the dead, had learned poetry as the young girls of the Andalusian aristocracy once did at the courts of Córdoba and Grenada. In a big house where she had been taken in because of her beauty, her masters had taught her, along with the young girls of the family, to compose rhymes, to sing, and to play the lute or the mandolin—opinion was divided as to which instrument it was. How had she come to this house? One night there was a persistent knocking at the studded door of the wealthy residence. Someone, for a period of time that seemed three times longer than it was because of the silence, had grabbed hold of the copper door knocker and was making it resound at regular intervals, without stopping. The watchman had peeked through the screened peephole before opening the door to a young girl who refused to answer any of his questions. At first, her silence roused curiosity. For several weeks it was thought that she was a poor deaf-mute, an orphan abandoned in a strange city, until one day she was found singing on the terrace where she slept alone on summer

[13]

nights. After that she was asked no more questions about her father and his family. The mistress of the house decided to educate her with her daughters, since she had enough servants. The stranger composed poems that she set to music along with the girls of the house, holding intimate concerts in the large hall that was decorated with mosaic tiles and where a gazelle, two peacocks, and some doves roamed freely, and where a patio, cooled by a green-and-blue fountain, was lighted by a large window. She spent several years in the beautiful house, until she disappeared on the day of her seventeenth birthday. The family took up a search that covered two hundred kilometers around the city, but in vain. The foundling never again knocked on the copper-studded door. The women at the baths argued over the truth about these obscure years when no one heard anything about the runaway, and then one day, they discovered that she was singing in a cabaret in the capital city. How could they be sure that it was indeed the same little girl who had been educated in the performing arts? Never for a moment did the women doubt the identity of the singer and musician performing in this famous house of pleasure to which people came from afar to hear the poems and music she composed for the lute and mandolin. What had happened? As the loving hands of the old women adorned the body of a young fiancée—a virgin whose white skin was now as hairless and smooth as the day she was born, for she was scrubbed, massaged, caressed, perfumed, and decorated as custom required—the women who were following the ritual revealed confidential stories linking the family home to a brothel, all the while contradicting one another. For some, the young girl had sought to escape a marriage she deemed unworthy of her. She was to be given to the favorite stable attendant of the master who owned a farm where he raised racehorses, but she was secretly in love with a cousin promised to one of the daughters of the house, a cousin she had spied from the terrace as he was saddling the

[14]

horses for the falcon hunt. They say she managed to join him near a fountain in a mountain village where the hunters water their horses, and then he reportedly carried her off, and they fled together. Since they were pursued, the cousin was presumed to have been killed, while she with no family, no home, is said to have used her artistic talents to earn a living in cabarets in the capital. According to another version told by some women in the baths, she returned on foot to her native village, to her maternal grandmother, who was still alive, the last member of a family decimated by a cholera epidemic, and she took care of her old blind grandmother, caring for her until she was buried, helped by two washers of the dead who taught her funeral litanies and who had met her a long time after her cabaret years. Did she frequent men like the other women in the group of musicians? The old women at the baths, the women who wash fiancées, say she did not. They ought to know. They often rented the bath to her privately. Her servants did not accompany her on those occasions. She would spend the day with the old masseuses, talking and eating the fruit they saved for her; she loved lime oranges and medlars most of all; she drank mint tea, and the old women would paint her feet and hands with red henna of the best quality and wash her hair with clay, squabbling over which one would take care of this body that was so white, firm, and plump. One of the masseuses, a former black slave, requested the privilege of washing her at the edge of the central bath, so the old women set out the fruit and tea on an embroidered table-cloth while the musician sat on silk cushions; the Negress fetched a lute, the old women stretched out on the tile floor to listen to her sing. That went on for years. The masseuses waited impatiently for the servant, who would come to notify them of the day the young woman wished to have the Moorish bath for herself. They would comb her hair in turns; her long black tresses were so thick, so heavy, that she said laughing to the women bustling around their creams that she, like the princess in an ancient poem she knew by heart, could braid her hair to form a rope for some forbidden lover to climb up from the steep road at the foot of the rampart to the terrace where she spent the night. But she promptly added that no man in this city was worthy of holding her hair. Someday, perhaps . . . she said, smoking the water pipe prepared by the Negress. She let herself be dressed by the old women, who admired her and lamented because she was not in love with anyone and would never have a husband or child, saying it was an offense to God not to follow her woman's destiny as wife and mother. She would smile, repeating that she preferred to compose poems and sing them for men and women in the street. She said she had turned down princely suitors and members of the royal family that still existed at that time. The old women believed only half of what she said. How could anyone refuse glory, luxury, and money? The old women did not know how to respond to women who asked them if she had ever been in love. She had not come for several weeks. One evening the Negress went alone to a famous nightclub where her name shone in gold letters, but she couldn't read the sign they were written on. She was told the singer had disappeared and that they had given up hope of seeing her again. Her name in gold letters was still on the sign, but for how long? The Negress came back to the baths in tears and told the two other masseuses that they would never again see the beautiful poetess. She picked up the lute from the bench and began to sing a poem of her native village that the old women had never heard. She sang all through the night and into the morning, then put the lute away in her trunk, where she had locked up her wedding trousseau forever. She hid the lute between two embroidered velvet dresses and was never heard singing again at the baths seated on the bench reserved for the poetess. For a long time the Negress looked for the missing girl. One night she was roaming in the street where the cabaret was located when the letters of another famous name were turned off, but she didn't know these letters weren't the same ones. She waited for the girl she would never see again. At the baths, she refused to wash the women or to massage them, accepting only one client because the girl reminded her of the one who had disappeared. She no longer worked or ate and was wasting away. People thought she had gone crazy. She spent all day sitting in front of the bathhouse door, waiting for the servant to announce the poetess's return. And then one night, her body was washed away by the river that had overflowed its banks, and she was never found again.

What is certain, say the women in the bathhouse who have heard the story of the musician and the Negress, is that the youngest of the three sisters who wash the dead is the little orphan girl, the famous singer who had neither lover nor child, a wanderer like her sisters, the two other women in black. People say they are sisters. They say the abandoned girl, the capricious poetess, found her sisters, who had taken refuge in a mountain cave on a winter evening, when she was dying of cold. Gossip has it that she recited a poem at the cave's entrance so that they would recognize her, and her elder sisters took her in. They have never separated since.

7

The sisters leave the house in mourning, flat cakes of the best quality have been prepared for them, they take with them lamb's cheese, figs, olive oil, and honey; they are being pampered so that they will never come back again; if they are treated badly, they could seek vengeance. They cross the fountainless courtyard enclosed by cactus bushes. The women watch them go off among the thick spiny leaves used to cover the child's tomb, protecting it against jackals. No one accompanies them; the children do not follow them as they would the itinerant musicians from the deep South who travel toward lands bordering the sea, welcomed, celebrated, honored, each household wishing to host two or three of them for several evenings, to host these tall, thin, black desert men who speak the language of the coast badly. Children love them; once a village boy ran off with them one dawn, a flute player who kept herds in the valley. He was never seen again. Did they adopt him? Perhaps he will come back, the only white man among the black musicians, wearing the same turban and the same loose-fitting garments held at the waist by a wide leather belt. His family would recognize him; he would sleep in his mother's house and go off again, roaming from village to village, on foot like the three sisters, but these men who came from so far away are happy men . . . The women in black walk through the only street in the village, alone; they speak among themselves in a whisper. Shutters open a crack as they go by; a curtain is raised behind a square window, doors creak as children whisper behind them, pushing one another for a view. The olive-wood cane taps against the pebbles on the road. The sisters skirt the wheat-covered hills as far as the river in the middle of the valley, then turn and join the narrow road lined with eucalyptus trees that leads to the ruins. They seat themselves far from the beehives and lavender shrubs, beside the wall of a sanctuary surrounded by cypress trees. It's summer, you can hear the sea. Children were searching for Roman coins to sell to collectors in the neighboring city; at the sound of the cane, they turned their heads toward the entrance of the Roman road; they saw the three sisters, who were coming toward them; the oldest children held the smallest in their arms and began running to the sea, jumping over rosemary bushes. Huddled against one another at the foot of the highest dune that separates the crumbling walls of the Roman city, they drew straws to find out which one of them the witches would carry off first. The game designated the youngest of them, a three-year-old boy who began to cry when his brother revealed his fate to him. The others burst out laughing, and the youngest imitated them. Upon reaching the port, the gang of boys thought they should tell the fishermen about the prediction that troubled them. The men, hunched over their nets, stood up, looked toward the ruins, where they had placed their beehives. The children told them the witches were several houses away from where the bees were. The fishermen continued repairing their nets, but one of them went to the ruins and guarded his hives until nightfall. He saw the sisters walk toward the foam, as was their custom; and when they stopped there, they washed their faces, hands, and forearms with sea water, then returned slowly toward the sanctuary that sheltered them for their last prayer. Leaning against the hives, he watched them prostrate themselves in prayer.

8

The fisherman recognizes the sisters. They have not died yet. They have not disappeared.

These same women had once come to the house where his mother died when the midwife couldn't save her. Instead of joyful ululations, he heard the cries and sobs of women frightened by the frantic gestures of the old midwife, who was unable to stop the hemorrhage. He was five years old then and had been kept away from his mother's room, where all the women were gathered. He waited, huddled against the fig tree in the courtyard as he is today, his back against the jetty wall as he repairs his nets. He saw women coming and going with steaming basins and blood-stained linen they were going to rinse in the small sink. They were heating water over a tripod guarded by a little cousin, who had sent him back to the fig tree when he tried to get close. She was helping the women, and what was he doing? He saw red water seeping out from under the door toward the ground in the courtyard. The yellow earth absorbed the water without turning red; he watched the bloody trickle for a long time, until he heard the women's first cry of distress. He had heard his mother moaning, had been told that giving birth to a child is painful; his cousin followed along with him the sounds of suffering echoed by the women around them, then he was no longer able to distinguish his mother's voice. He had gotten up; a neighbor explained that everything was going well, that the baby was coming, he must be patient. He sat down against the tree, waited, and saw the blood mixed with water that made a brown spot like clear water soaked into the earth. You could no longer tell it was water mixed with a woman's blood that was coming from the room where the women had begun to scream. He ran to the door. The women surrounded his mother's bed, the big bed where he sometimes slept with his mother, lying next to her firm round stomach on summer afternoons when it was too hot for him to go down to the river to fish or to search for crabs hiding under the rocks. He didn't see his little brother, the stillborn child, nor his mother because of the women, giants as heavy as the statues in the Roman ruins, immovable beings who kept him from seeing his mother and brother. He tried to slip between the folds of their skirts, crawling on the wet reddened tile floor, but he was pushed back violently. One of his aunts, the sturdiest, took him in her arms like an infant and carried him away from the room and the sobs, clasping him against her large soft breasts, and he said—Mama, Mama—several times as his aunt's tears fell on his arms, he wasn't crying—he kept saying—Mama—his aunt was silent. She sat down against a wall, in the shade, holding him in the folds of her skirt like a tiny infant one rocks and comforts with a lullaby; but she wasn't singing, she was crying softly, and he began to suck his thumb. He awoke when the three sisters arrived, the oldest walking without a cane. It was he who screamed upon seeing them standing next to one another, draped in their somber veils and headscarves and moving toward his mother's room. His aunt rose, ran toward the women, and kissed their foreheads before showing them into the room he had not been allowed to enter. His aunt came toward him, took him in her arms as she wrapped him in her veil; he felt hot underneath her veil but said nothing. She put on her city shoes and went out. They sat at the edge of the ruins, and with the pebbles she collected they made a wall almost as tall as he was; he wasn't afraid, he said that even if pirates rushed out of the sea to attack him, he wouldn't die. That evening, the witches were still in his mother's room, so he slept at a neighbor's house and did so for several nights until they left. When he went back to his house, the witches had taken away his mother and brother, and he didn't see them again until this day as he watches them saying their final prayer at night.

9

They cannot see the fisherman. Are they going to stay there for a long time? He is suddenly worried about his bees. The next day he returns to the spot at the ruins where the sisters have their house that opens onto the sky. They aren't there. Before they return he leaves them a pot of honey and a pot of milk on the solid ledge of the sanctuary. His wife is raising a goat in their courtyard behind the house down by the port that his father left for him. He had made pots with the other village children. They would collect clay, and the women would give them the paint for the brown and black geometric designs. The children would then give them to the baker to be fired. He kept several of the pots his children hadn't broken; they try to sell them to foreigners strolling under the eucalyptus trees on the square. As soon as he glimpses the sisters on the other side of the road, walking through the grapevines—the grapes aren't ripe yet— the fisherman returns to the village and the game of dominoes he had interrupted. Everyone knows the sisters are there in their city of ruins that the children have abandoned. People wonder how long they will stay in the ancient city and whom they have come for. The boldest boys set up watch for several nights not far from the cemetery, hidden by the trunk of an ancient olive tree. Some boys stay behind at the tree until dawn. They say the oldest sister digs up the dead with her cane and that she keeps hair, teeth, and even fingers ripped from corpses hidden in a goatskin pouch. Then, sheltered by the ruins, the sisters mix up a potion of dead frogs and snakes, which they store in jars they bury in the cemetery, along with powder they make from plants they collected in the hills. People have seen them coming back with armfuls of herbs they then crush in a mortar. They have heard the sound of the pestle at various times, the same sound their mothers make pounding grain, cumin, hot peppers, and coriander; but the witches they are spying on make evil ointments and brews. The boys say nothing about this to their mothers, but they gossip with their sisters and girl cousins, putting them on guard against these magicians. When the boys talk about this, they touch the small hand of Fatma they wear around their necks, hidden under their T-shirts. The girls don't follow them as far as the cemetery. They wait at the edge of the village, playing a form of hopscotch using a pebble or a tin of chewing tobacco. The fisherman enter the big house where the fountain is now dry, where there are cracks in the pillars and the terrace. The women are anxious. He goes toward his sister, the one who hasn't received any money orders from her husband for years. She is speaking with her distant husband's mother; and what if the three sisters were waiting for him to return in order to have him die . . . She doesn't put it quite that way. Who could possibly speak of the death of the absent son to his mother, who could possibly do that? Unless it was to bring misfortune upon oneself; no, she isn't saying that, but the women in black are so close to the village . . . She's heard people say that wherever they stop misfortune occurs. Why would it happen to her or the husband who no longer lives with her? They also say that the sisters sense impending death from a distance. But there is a sea between the two shores; isn't water a barrier? They use air to sense death; they have been seen huddled around a tripod where they burn herbs mixed with powdered bones, and smoke has been seen rising above the ruins. The sisters read smoke rings, studying the form, direction, odor of the smoke; if it heads toward the sea, it's a sign that misfortune will be coming from across the sea. Of the many men who have been gone all these years, which husband, brother, cousin will not return as young and strong as the day he left? The fisherman approaches his sister, the cousin with the blond curly hair, whispering to her about his offering to the three sisters. Before leaving, he gives her a pot of honey; she looks at the saffron-colored honey and says that her children love their uncle's honey, but he doesn't answer. He gently closes the green door of the big house. Her brother told her when the sisters wash their feet, face, and hands in sea water; their ablutions take a long time, so she has nothing to fear. But she knows what people have been saying, those who prowl around the ruins and the cemetery. She won't go there at dusk, alone. Her brother has warned her to stay away and not let herself be caught by the sisters when she is all alone. The fumigations continue, and no one understands the incantations in a secret language that each person translates in his own way. Supposedly people can recognize some names, when they are repeated several times, but no one says which ones. She has made some wheat cakes; the children were down at the port—they would have begged to eat some—the other women said nothing. Before sunrise, she picked the first fig flowers. She left for the ruins with the wheat cakes, the figs, and the honey wrapped in a white cloth, the offering hidden under her veil. She knows where the sanctuary is. It is there that she and the girls her age once set up their

[23]

playhouse, which was off limits to the boys unless they had received an official invitation. With Roman stones they had dug up, the girls had built a room where they grilled the fish the boys brought to please them. One day the girls screamed in fright because a boy had thrown a live octopus into their cabin made of olive branches onto the floor covered with long eucalyptus leaves. She remembers how the twisted tentacles beat against the fragile walls of the house propped up against the sanctuary; the monster was going to destroy the house and strangle the little girls crouched against the wall. That day they abandoned the site, the sea animal was a bad omen, she can still see the gigantic black octopus spewing its sticky ink. In addition, that very evening her mother warned her that from then on she must stay in the big house, since she had passed the age of running around with the other children. Since then, she has never gone back to the ancient Roman city. She follows the crumbling walls along the side of the road to get to the cemetery or the Moorish bath once a week, or the family marabout's tomb on the third hill over from the cemetery. She walks quickly. She has put on a new veil that doesn't look at all like the others. Several yards from the sanctuary, she sees a thin waft of smoke at the very spot where as a little girl she and the others grilled onions and fish before the incident of the octopus. She stops, looks toward the sea. The sisters are standing upright facing the somber waves. She hurries. She avoids walking on the worn mats, goes around the smoking tripod, places the honey, flat wheat cakes, and figs on the edge of a wide flat stone. She has just enough time to fold the linen she didn't want to leave behind when she hears a murmur and the sound of the cane. She hides behind the carob trees. If she can hear them, she may be able to find out they are not predicting the death of her absent husband. She stays there for a long time, but the sisters say no more. They pray, turning their mats in the appropriate direction for their sea-water ablutions, eat a little bit of

[24]

the cake; each one takes a fig, they drink the fisherman's milk, and they lie down. Just harmless old women, punctual, efficient washers of the dead, and all those rumors . . . She learned nothing. The sisters have fallen asleep like children. Tomorrow they will be gone. There will be no death in the village, nor across the sea on the other shore. She returns to the big house, walking along the beach, barefoot in the sand, skirting the edge of the foam; she lifts one side of her dress, fastening it in her belt at the place where she tucks in her veil. At the bend in the small creek she glimpses the port. It is night. Although it's summer, she shivers. Suddenly, she is startled by the sound of a long shrill cry. She stops, standing against the rock near the port. Where is the cry coming from? The ruins? The village? She listens, flattened against the rock, trembling. There are lights on in the windows of the houses facing the sea. The cry seems to roll with the waves, it is less shrill, continuous. It is coming from the foreign shore. She starts to run, pursued by the scream, she pushes on the green door, collapses at the foot of the dry fountain, the women have awakened, her mother-in-law is the first. They listen, standing around the fountain where the woman lies in tears—it's my son—say the mothers—it's my husband . . . it's my brother . . . it's my father . . . The fisherman dresses quickly. He runs to his sister's house, where he sees the women lamenting on the patio with the cracked mosaic tiles. They wait for him to speak. In a hushed voice he says that the women from the ruins are heading for the village; he does not know which house they will stop at. The women fall silent, glued to the spot. The fisherman leaves, he must protect his family. But who will protect them, the women in the old house that is decaying further with each passing day? Only God. The men are no longer there. Some return, others don't, and those who come back stay just a few weeks. They spend the nights with their wives; they don't want to spend their days repairing the house; they play dominoes or take fishing boats out to

[25]

sea; they say they need to rest, they need to restore their strength for the next voyage, the next job. The youngest woman opens the door, the neighbors also listen for the sound of the cane; they can hear it coming from the end of the street; the blond-haired cousin returns to the patio in despair; the women wait, huddled together against the fountain. When the three sisters arrive at the green door, it is locked. The oldest sister raps with her cane.

I O

On the other shore, in the white room, the man who used to walk by the river is dying.

II

At the bend in the river, he fell.

Who will speak my mother's words to me?

In the white room where I am alone, who will come to whisper the prayer of the dead? And who will whisper in my ear in the language of my homeland, in the silence of the other shore?

I

The man who walks along the riverbank has repeated so often that he never thinks of his death, that it doesn't interest him. His body can be left wherever he dies . . . on an arid hill where jackals shriek, or on the side of a six-lane highway between trash cans overflowing with Coca-Cola cans, partially empty beer cans that will hit him in the head, and paper cups stained with women's lipstick; it could be on a distant jetty in the evening when the fish have stopped biting but he doesn't feel like leaving—the others have already left the foot of the lighthouse, taking their pails with them, whether they are full of fish or empty, and bringing the bottles of sea water the women in the family had asked for. Or it could be in a café where men, afraid of their homes and the women in them, come to spend part of the night. At closing time, they walk in the dead city or along the port. They never leave in groups, even though they have talked and played cards or dominoes together for hours on end. His head will hit the counter or the table, and his glass still full of beer will spill all over the clothes of the person standing next to him who will yell at him before realizing the man has suddenly died. He may have said jokingly to his evening companions that no arrangements have been made for him, that he is only a poor devil, and they can throw his corpse into a common grave, where he will join his brothers of misfortune, his brothers in life and at the bar, his brothers in death, poets like himself. And what about them? They say there will always be a small place left for him, once his father's or grandfather's remains have been rearranged; the women take care of these things . . . And he says his body will be tossed into the desert, the common grave where you are all alone, without your family or anything, all alone in the desert, with the ever-shifting sand, where a tomb disappears as the wind blows and the dunes shift. You can never mark anything on it. What use would that be? Who would read the erased letters? You have to die near cities or villages, places where the sand is trapped by clumps of thorny bushes, trees, tombstones, and palm trees.

2

His mother was speaking to him, to the fellow making fun of his own death; he heard her repeat the words he has never forgotten. She was still young, and they were living in the big house he left so many years ago . . . He has never been back, never . . . His youngest brother, the one he convinced to come without his wife, their blond curly-haired cousin—he could never find lodging for his family—well, he learned about him by accident, since they no longer saw each other because of a quarrel over money. The brother came back to the village in a sealed casket, back to the big house, the sea and the ruins, and the three sisters, who were there the very day he arrived . . . His mother never stopped talking about her own death, frightening the other women of the house. Only he would listen to her, on washdays, and he promised he would never forget her words, he would carry out her request and would chase away the women in black, those witches, so they would not touch her. He would be there to bar the women's entrance to her bedroom and make sure that her youngest grandchild, still a virgin, the daughter of her seventh son and their cousin, would be there in the house to watch over her. Just before her death, the granddaughter would whisper in her ear the prayers for the dead, reciting them alone, at her side. She will not be afraid; her grand-daughter, her very favorite was told about this a very long time ago. The voice of the prettiest, most sensitive young girl in her family, a voice so serene and pure, almost as if it came from heaven, that's what she wants to hear. Her oldest son will be there. Why would he leave the house, which is beautiful once more; he will know what to do, as will his wife. She keeps no secret from her grandchild; she knows everything. When the oldest son was still a child he made a promise, because he always said yes to his mother. How she loved him. And then he left. He didn't say a word. He left the big house and the village forever, and many years have passed now. He knows nothing of the village, or his mother, or whether she has died . . . The sisters in black, he knows them. He would spy on them, with the boys in his gang, each time they came back to their city in ruins. Here, on the foreign shore, he has seen them in strange places, the three women in black, three sisters sitting on benches in a square or on metal park chairs, three old women sitting on steps leading down to the sea. They must have passed on before his mother. He would have heard if something had happened to his mother; you always find out about these things by chance. He is sure she has prepared the young girl, the youngest person living in the big house. She also told him how the worthiest men die, and that he should die that way. She told him everything. He knows all about it, and if he speaks his mind, talking the way he does at café counters in the foreign land where he'll die, it is not because of his mother, it is because of his life. His beer-drinking buddies listen to the man from the Roman city who keeps insisting if you live like a dog you die like a dog, and that's all you deserve. His own life hasn't been any better than that. His mother is waiting for him, and he knows why. He won't return to the village alive. In the café, they tell him to forget the three sisters from the ruins, those harbingers of death who prowl around villages young people have left. Speaking of these very old women, dressed all in black and alert, the young folks say they trade life for death. Is that true? The young take off, letting the village go to wrack and ruin. You see the old women in the cemeteries. Who knows what they are doing, but since they are the oldest ones, nobody objects. Maybe they are keeping the graves tidy. Who still comes to pray? Even on the day of the dead, they are the only ones who walk down the paths with wheelbarrows and watering cans. But he talks on and on; the café is going to close. It is late; the others in the city have already closed their shutters; the café owner puts the chairs up on the tables. Standing at the counter, alone in the night, the man speaks in his childhood tongue, the language he spoke before he went to school, the language spoken in the big house in those happy days before the men deserted it, when their voices still joined in with the women's. The sisters were still far away, and the old woman had not taken her aunt's cane. The café owner sweeps up the fresh cigarette butts at his feet, the wrinkled cigarette papers, stubs from racetrack bets, torn bus tickets, and sausage skins. He says he's waiting two more years and then he'll move into the house he is building on the land he inherited back home in his village. He speaks softly, like the man standing there who is raising first one foot and then the other as the café owner passes with his broom; he can't understand the foreign language. Suddenly he stops in his tracks; the guy has asked him where he wants to be buried. He answers that it's not the time for somber thoughts and that he too should get some sleep. In four hours it will be daylight.

The man walks by the river, this first day of summer, heading for the spot where he likes to fish. The river leads to the sea; he follows it. It is Sunday morning. In a day he can walk down to the sea without getting exhausted. He will find a fishing line at the port. He prefers his own, always the same one. He will not go to his wife's house at this hour. He doesn't think of it as his house as well as hers. The house belongs to his wife, the fishing rod to him. No one touches it, or his cap either. As for the rest . . . The coffee is his; he buys it, and his wife makes his coffee when he is there. He glimpses a man on the other shore walking toward the sea like himself, smoking corn-paper Gitanes, he can tell by the way the man is inhaling without taking the cigarette out of his mouth. When he fishes, he smokes corn-paper Gitanes so he won't be distracted. The man wears a fisherman's cap, unlike him. He prefers a checkered cap, the kind you find in this region at the Friday morning market. They walk at the same pace. They will meet up at the next seaside café in time for the pari-mutuel. What he wins at the races he bets on cards, and what he wins at cards he drinks with his friends, men with rough hands. They left their sterile homeland for machines and mines, following in the footsteps of those who went to war, who were the first on the front lines in the other land where the soil is thick and heavy. The names of their fallen soldiers were not etched on village war monuments. His companions forgot how to write, but not he. He writes letters for fathers, husbands, brothers, cousins . . . He writes for each one's household; the oldest son who goes to school will read the letter he writes for all of them. Attentive, the men watch him write. He writes quickly on blue-lined paper. There are many who confide their secrets to him, the same from one letter to another. He has become a public scribe. His friends invite him to eat and sleep at their homes; he sometimes accepts their hospitality. He doesn't work in the mines or the giant factories called "witches" by the men he plays dominoes with, just as they do in the cafés of his home village and on the terraces shaded by fig trees.

He writes poems and walks along the river. Sometimes he reads poems aloud in both languages. His friends listen, often for hours. They drink beer and say nothing when he stops speaking. He folds the blue-lined sheets of paper he writes on and tucks them into his inside jacket pocket. Sometimes he writes on the edge of an embossed paper tablecloth and then forgets to take the slip of paper with him. He passes solitary men sitting silently on green wooden benches facing the river. They stare at the dirty ground at their feet. They don't look at the river. They are waiting for the racing results. He didn't stop at the same time as the other man, at the first café to open on Sunday. He knows them all, particularly the one he found a few years ago by the shore. It also sells fishing gear and newspapers. He found fishing lures he had never seen anywhere else, next to newspapers and a rack of paperback books, and in the back, fishing boots and plastic raincoats. He told the owner that if, by chance, he were to die suddenly—no, he is not ill—but a fortune-teller told him his death will be quick; he won't suffer, he won't know what hit him—the proprietor shouldn't worry. He's alone, with no family, no one to contact anywhere. They should grab his feet, drag him down to the jetty, and toss him into the sea. This is the first time he has said this to anyone. The café owner is a wise man; he can tell him his last wish. Okay, he heard him, he has to promise. They must seal the pact with a firm handshake, palm against palm, right hand against right hand. It has to be the right hand, otherwise the pact is invalid. He had better be sure the café owner isn't left-handed. They aren't going to shake hands for nothing. His last wish must be respected. He doesn't need to put it in writing. The café owner has agreed, and he trusts him; he repeats his last wish one more time.

He didn't tell him he writes poetry.

3

At home, in the seaside village, his plot is reserved, his mother has told him this many times. He is next to her and his grandmother in the maritime cemetery in the shade of the marabout's tomb. He won't go into the village beside the Roman ruins. Some cousins came looking for him. Since he had left no address they searched in vain for a long time. But one Sunday when he was at the café where he placed his bets, the only one that was already open on the village square—he knows it so well because of the river teeming with fish—there, someone called his name from the door; he saw his cousin standing there, hands outstretched toward him. They played the horses. He won and gave his cousin money for his mother but refused to give more when his cousin talked about the house that needed repairing, and the fountain that wasn't working, and the pillars about to collapse. He said no, he wouldn't come home. He sends money to his mother so she can pay the masons. There are very competent masons back home, and they know more than he does. The cousin kept trying to persuade him, right up to the moment they parted, and he left with the crumpled bills in his jacket pocket. The cousin had even confirmed his mother was sick and that she was asking for him. He refused to believe it, convinced his mother wasn't ill and that she never talks about him. He knows that's the case; he told his cousin he had been to see a magician from their village, a woman who had tried to track down her husband. She had his address on an envelope, but when she arrived there, she realized he had tricked her. It was a false address. She didn't find him and didn't want to alert the police for

[33]

fear of being expelled. She stayed on, working in the red-light district. He recognized her one night in a bar and promptly left. He didn't want to hear about the village, the house, and his mother. And one day, by chance—for everything in his life happens by chance—he was at a fair and walked into a fortune-teller's trailer. Her name was Soraya. The sign was decorated with badly painted arabesques, but he liked her name. He didn't say anything, nor did she. But she talked about the hillside where she was born, the courtyard surrounded by Barbary fig bushes, and the harvest day when the sisters, the three of them, arrived at night to take away the body of the little cousin killed by a blow from a horse's hoof. She spoke of her sorrow at not being allowed to accompany the body to the cemetery below, of the Fridays when she accompanied the women who tended the little grave, giving water to the birds and watering the flowers planted around the tomb. When sitting with the veiled women, she wore a headscarf. She would listen to them talk. They said she shouldn't go into the ruins near the eucalyptus trees because the three sisters kidnap children there. The fortune-teller spoke about his mother, her frequent visits to the marabout, the charms she strung on the branches of the sacred tree to protect the son who lived so far away, the son she hadn't seen for years, the son who would not keep his promise . . .

The man interrupts the fortune teller. She assures him his mother isn't ill, that she loves the son who left her and doesn't curse him. She told him she would warn him as soon as she saw the women from the ruins prowling near the big house. That day he gave her all the money he had, and she swore she would keep him informed, even if he doesn't come back to see her. Every time he consults Soraya she tells him the truth. He has spent a lot of money in the trailer at the fair held twice a year. He knows where to find it, but last summer Soraya wasn't there. Perhaps she changed her name or her trailer. He walked around the spot where the fortune-tellers meet on the esplanade called "The Way of the Future." The seven magicians told him more about his death than about his life. Soraya disappeared, and he never saw her again. If he walks along the river to the sea, this summer Sunday, if he doesn't spend all his money on the races, on cards, and on beer and takes the boat, he can go straight to the village port, where he will find out that Soraya no longer goes by that name, that she has bought a little white house next door to the fisherman's house. It is whitewashed with blue trim to protect it from being eaten away by sea water, and at the edge of the wall she has planted basil in blue pots to ward off the evil eye. He doesn't stop at the seaside café where he usually spends his Sundays when he sets out at dawn, returning on foot at night, sometimes bringing home fish. He hasn't found a boat seaworthy enough to cross the sea to Soraya's house. If he had, she would see him arrive just in time; he would have heard her call; she had promised to alert him, never to lie to him, especially the day he absolutely has to keep the sisters from heading for the old house, from coming up to the rusty green front door. It hasn't been repainted for a very long time, the rust makes lacy holes at the bottom and on the sides. He runs. The sisters have already left the ruins; he takes a shortcut to get there before them, to bar their passage. He will kill them if he has to. They are old and feeble. His mother must never see them. He doesn't run as well as he used to. He was always the winner and was considered a future champion, a long-distance runner, although he never believed it. He wasn't cut out to be a marathoner. When he arrives at the big ramshackle house, the front door is open, and he sees the sisters moving toward the women huddled near the dried-up fountain. In the port, the boats are fragile; he can see them through the café window facing the sea.

4

The man lost at dominoes because of the women chatting at the next table, the café owner's wife, her sisters, and her friends. They knit while the woman tends the store. They talk louder and louder so she can hear them from her booth when a client comes in. One of the women has just returned from the cemetery behind the abandoned factory. The red-and-black brick chimney is more resistant than the workshops. It watches over the dead at its feet. The woman says it shouldn't be torn down. It's like a lighthouse but without a light at night. Still, it's a kind of beacon; the sea breeze blows through the factory's broken windows down to the cemetery, smelling of algae. She recognizes the smell of her husband's boat, a trawler she went out to sea on with him more than once. She decorated the grave with shells and wrote her husband's name with round white pebbles. She has her place reserved next to his. Their children are grown now, except for the youngest one still living at home. She has plenty of time. With her jars full of shells and pebbles she has been collecting since she was a child, she sits at her table on the balcony, the one that needs repainting because of the sea air. Looking out at the sea and the boats, she writes his name under the flower bouquet she designed with gray and black pebbles and mostly white shells. Her daughter says it's gloomy, but she's certainly not going to use colors on a grave . . . She hesitated when she saw colored varnished pebbles, because they hold up better in bad weather, but her taste tends more to subdued decoration. She quickly adds the missing date, showing it to her daughter, who objects every time she talks about it; but she rarely asks her anything; she uses the pebbles she has saved to write a date, four numbers. For her husband, she begins to draw a trawler. She knows a mason who will be able to engrave it on the tombstone. He will do the same for her. She works at this project when she's alone; her daughter doesn't like to see her working at epitaphs. Birds come and go, flying in formation past the café window; judging from their thin pointed wings, they must be swallows. The man playing dominoes stops, listens to the birds squawking. Their cry is too shrill for them to be swallows, and their undercoat is black.

A swallow's nest is up against the ceiling, atop the patio pillars. Grandmother insisted it not be destroyed. The women were permitted to chase away the other swallows because of their droppings, but the nest remained. When he saw the first swallow, he called his grandmother, and together they watched the work. His grandmother said she'd seen the same swallow among the vines at the edge of a puddle. It was cleaning off the mud before choosing a piece of straw; the wheat field on the hill is not far away. Alone, day after day, the mother bird made the round walls of the nest perched up there. His grandmother said the swallow's nest would outlive him. The men who left the house and returned sometimes two or three years later, they would recognize the nest she'd been protecting since the birth of her grandson. She told him he was born the same day as the baby swallows of the first nest. She added that his wooden cradle with the straw mattress was less comfortable than that of the baby swallows who lay on white feathers. Grandmother said it seems the mother birds only liked clean white feathers and refused the others. He watched over the swallow and its white feathers, fine soft feathers, baby chick's down. His grandmother told the truth. He didn't wait, as he had every year, for the first swallow to nest atop the pillar when he left his grandmother's house. Soraya, in her trailer, will tell him at the next fair that the nest hasn't been destroyed and that the swallows return faithfully. He looks at the birds that are not swallows. The women are talking too loudly; he doesn't want to hear them. It's the time of day when he stops fishing. Before going back along the riverbank, he tries to win a game of dominoes, just for fun. He's no longer distracted by the birds. Do these birds that look like swallows come here from across the sea, from the far-off tip of Africa? These migrants never lose their way; they know where they are going, but he knows nothing about where he should live. He just follows chance and destiny, not like the swallows, who never veer off their course. He never chased birds in the ruins or around the hills. He made sling-shots out of grenadine wood, the most supple hardwood. He called it his marine slingshot. When he walks alone along the riverbank, he sometimes throws pebbles in the water, sometimes really far, as if he had a slingshot.

6

Laughing, the women sitting and knitting suggest their neighbor work for them; each one of them would order her favorite flower—in colors, otherwise it is too sad—with her initials resembling the em-broidered linen of a trousseau. A sheet of paper torn from the café owner's order book is passed around. The neighbor says they have to simplify certain letters. They all know where their burial plot will be. The length of time a family owns a plot is becoming shorter, espe-cially in large cities, where cemeteries can't get any larger. Here, you don't have to worry. The family has the plot for life, until the world comes to an end. Then, what with atomic warfare, the whole world will turn to dust, perhaps like the first day of the world, when the earth had no people, at the beginning. But what you need is a family vault, the plot of course, but never just the earth. Even the most weather-resistant coffin collapses under the weight of the earth, mix-ing everything up, the mud and the rest of it. One of them was present at the reduction of her husband's father's body. In this family they don't have a family vault. They are just put in the ground; it is not a pretty sight. She was happy to have a vault, a place for her husband, even if he is not part of the family. They had both names engraved for the children, it's better that way . . . The bones are placed in a little coffin. You have to wait five years before requesting the reduction; but if the vault is made for four, it is not meant for eight; that is what she was told. She saved up for herself, but her husband's death came suddenly. She had to empty her savings account, and now, slowly, she's building it up again. The children will have nothing to pay, not like in some families that don't want to think about it and put nothing aside—neither the parents nor the children—and then they end up in the pauper's grave . . . They don't even get a tombstone, so nobody knows who's buried there; there's no name, no dates; the person never existed. It's as if the person died far away from home and has no one to take care of his remains . . . All these young people, she remembers a TV program she saw several years ago; they were almost children, abandoned corpses lying there for several days, their helmets askew, in those desert regions. They were still wearing their white headbands with red inscriptions in honor of their God. Their shoes had been ripped off. For miles, the survivors stepped over dead bodies; they were the same age but didn't have time for those lying on the ground and perhaps not even time to remove their identification papers from the inside pocket of their military vest and send them to their families, to identify the martyr and allow them to believe the soldier hadn't been left to the hyenas. So his mother could mourn him, and his name could be engraved on the monument honoring the young warriors; he would not be all alone, so far away in the mud and the stones, offering his bare hands against the bombers. He had gone off with the others, singing or rather shouting to God's glory. He was told that if he died, he would find his place at God's right hand. He thought this was true and that his death would be a glorious one, provided his mother were to get his hero's pension, compensation for what she had spent to make him a patriotic soldier, a soldier of God. So often, she saw pictures of these boys in their soldiers uniforms, lying dead in rocky trenches and alone, with nothing around them except the empty desert. She thought of her sons, even though they are not at war here, and what she would do, what she would say. She would put medals of Saint

[39]

Christopher and the Virgin Mary around their necks, medals she keeps in a cookie tin with her other gold jewelry at the bottom of a sewing basket under the socks waiting to be darned. And when she goes away for two or three days, she buries the tin wrapped in several plastic bags to protect it from metal detectors in a deep hole under the kitchen window, covering the ground with old tiles that have been there forever. Along with these medals that no robber would ever want she placed the baby bracelets against one another, the ones they put on her newborn babies' wrists at the hospital. Her mother gave birth at home, attended by an old midwife from the region, but not she. By then, the old woman was too old and lived in a remote village. Women who go to see her say her plants and her prayers have magic powers . . . The nurses wrote the first name, the last name, and the date of birth of each one of her children on those bracelets. She didn't discard them, nor did she throw away their baby teeth, keeping them all together in a sturdy hardwood box. She can't say who they belong to, but what matters is that she can find them whenever she wants to. What use is that? She doesn't know. It's just that she has never been able to throw them away. She hasn't lost them. The morning after the tooth fairy came she looked for the tooth under the pillow so she could put it away with the others just as her mother had done. Her mother has passed away, but she knows where her box is with all its contents: the jewelry, the baby teeth, the locks of hair, the letters written from the front. Mother was engaged at that time; she burned them a few days before she died. As long as her mother's grandmother was alive, she was the one who took care of the baby teeth. They left that task to her. She said it was better to hide them under the stones of the front doorstep of the house or in the cemetery wall—certainly not to throw them in the fire—so they could surely be found on Resurrection Day. She believed that. She would give the children a coin in exchange for the tooth. After her death, they put the teeth in the holes in the fireplace or in the walls of the house, the children having fun looking for the coin. But now in their family they put the tooth under the pillow or under a glass in the cupboard as they do in her husband's family. In their family, now the custom has been lost, and so no one knows who took the rings and the pendants —they used to have the fiancé or fiancée's first baby tooth made into a ring. But these days, baby teeth have been replaced by pearls that shine more brightly. Still, it's a shame it isn't done anymore. She would love to have had a ring made of baby teeth . . . The first locks of baby hair she cut she placed in a locket. She can't say today whose locks of hair they are. She didn't think to write the name of each child, boy or girl, on a small piece of paper in the locket. She could try to identify them by color, but the children have never asked for them, not even the lockets. If her sons were going to war, like the children in the Orient, she would make them wear them. The oldest had already objected once because she gave him the Saint Christopher's medal, making him promise to wear it around his neck, not while he was living in barracks in his own country during his military service, but if he were sent to war in Africa, the Gulf, or elsewhere. He promised he would, but he never left the military camp in the neighboring city. The children must know her last wishes. She has told them about the family vault, the money in her account, the checkbook hidden in the soup tureen. They know about her clothes, the tweed suit she wore for her engagement. She tried it on a few days ago; it hasn't gone out of style, and she hasn't gained weight since she was twenty. One day, her daughter, the one who still lives with her, saw her in front of the closet mirror in her bedroom. She began to laugh before trying the suit on herself. The skirt would have to be lengthened, and so she decided not to give it to her daughter. And when she showed her the place in the closet where she kept it with other clothes, the white piqué blouse, the shoes and shiny stockings, the rosary for her hands, her daughter asked for nothing more. She understood that until her mother's death, these clothes would stay in the same spot in the closet, in a corner on the left-hand shelf, next to the love letters. She hadn't yet decided if she should leave them for her daughters or burn them just before she dies. One Sunday when they were all having lunch at the house, when none of them were married yet—she rarely sees them together now—she made them listen to Gregorian chants. She didn't immediately tell them why. They promised to have these chants sung during the church service, before going to the cemetery and during the masses that would be said for their mother. They promised to do it, and she explained everything to her youngest daughter: the jewelry, the bank account, the special account, the clothing, the letters—she is at peace. She often told her husband that a family vault is better, more dignified. He would tease her, saying that when you are dead, you are dead, vault or no vault. She didn't like him joking about this, talking like a nonbeliever. Once he even said, and he wasn't joking, that he would like to have his ashes strewn at sea. He had seen ashes strewn in the desert on TV. She can't remember the hero's name, but her husband told the story for several days in a row, saying he too would like to return to ashes, purified by fire and given to the sea. She cried so that he would change his mind about losing his soul this way. He never had the time to express his last wishes, and now the Church allows cremation. She buried her husband as a true Christian. Her children will bury her as a Christian among Christians; she has no doubt about that. The man playing dominoes listens to the women. His partners, men who speak his native language and who drink a lot of beer like him, especially on Sundays, fuss because he's playing badly. If they win, it's because he's not paying attention. They ask him what he finds in these French women who are neither young nor beautiful and are even more talkative than their wives. At least the women at

[42]

home know to keep quiet in front of men, and the men watch their words in the presence of women. In the café, the women are speaking too loudly, and all the men, not only the foreigners, can hear what they are saying to one another, things men shouldn't know. They want no part of this, but men here, even if they don't listen to the women, let them talk in front of people they don't know, clients passing through, fishermen who stop by before returning to their camping cars and the dinners their wives have prepared for them at the riverbank, unemployed city youths on Sunday outings with their girlfriends, migrant workers waiting for the evening bus to take them back to the farms in the country, and the men playing dominoes who are annoyed at winning so easily.

7

The three sisters were said to leave the ruins at night to wander among the abandoned houses on the hills, searching for what the women, before leaving on their final journey, had left behind in the walls or buried in inner courtyards, at the bottom of wells, in fountain basins, and at the foot of trees. They never went looking for silver or gold. At the baths, the women told so many stories. Should we believe them? Boys who were still little would accompany their mothers on bath days. He went with his mother, grandmother, and the women of the house, but not all of them went. Some stayed in their rooms, but he didn't know why. He almost cried the day his mother forbade him to go to the women's baths; but she was insistent, congratulating him because from now on he would go along with the men; he didn't cry. Mothers washed their daughters' hair with clay, combing their hair for a long time. They would hold the hair on combs the girls would ask for at the end of the ritual, that only those girls whose hair was too curly to flatter a mother's pride would escape. He remembers his little cousin seated on the stone bench. She was crying, tortured by friends pulling her hair to make it longer, straighter. She was blond and thought herself ugly because her hair would never be straight. Her mother always said—My daughter has blond hair that is shiny but curly. Did someone one day tell her her hair is prettier when, at the end of the day at the bath, it dries in little ringlets on her forehead and curls down her neck and shoulders? But she pulled her hair back, flattening it under a tight headscarf that wouldn't let the smallest strand escape. If he had ever spoken to her about her hair, she would have thought he was teasing. In any case, it never occurred to him to tell her that her hair was beautiful—a boy never speaks like that to a girl, not even if she's his cousin. He often saw her with other girls looking for the clearest and swiftest rivulets to toss the clump of matted hair into—to watch it unravel and straighten out in the stream of running water, but hers stayed curled as she followed it to the edge of the village, and the other girls made fun of her disappointment.

The girls repeated these secret rituals every time their mothers washed and combed their long tresses. The boys knew about this and watched them from afar, spying on them. Mothers forbade their daughters to leave their hair in the rivulets. Where would it end up? Someone might get hold of it, and then who knows what might happen. The sisters living in the ruins were looking for the hair of virgins, and not only their hair but everything you can remove from a body without hurting it, including bathwater, the dirty water containing hair and dead skin. Women warned the girls of the sterile old magicians' jealousy and their malevolence toward young girls of marriageable age. Mothers advised them to throw their nail clippings into the fire, certainly not to leave them anywhere. It was rumored that the black crows raised by the sisters collect nail clippings in their beaks and leave them on a hollow stone at the foot of the sanctuary the sisters occupied when they were in the mood. Once they moved into the ruins, no one knew when they would leave. The sisters would grind the nails that resembled the beaks of certain birds, mixing them with roots they collected in the valley, flower seeds, sand from the dunes, jackal livers, hyena intestines. To that they added hair collected in the water flowing in streams far from the village and, if they were able to get them, baby teeth. That is what the women told one another at the baths, warning the children they couldn't do just anything. Their mothers were vigilant, but could they guard against outside dangers? When the children were still little, they cut their nails short, repeating that long dirty nails protect the devil, immediately throwing the clippings into the embers. But what happened when they no longer stayed at home, and their sons' hands escaped their watch? Then, they used threats, what more could they do? They piously put aside the first lock of hair the day the barber came to the house for the boys of the family once they were no longer babies and, with it, the first baby tooth. The man losing at dominoes throws coins into the middle of the table. Speaking in his native tongue, he tells the men he plays and drinks with that even if he is stripped as bare as a beggar, they will never get the gold coins his mother is keeping for him. He knows she has them but doesn't know where. He was bleeding the day he lost his first tooth and spit. It was red; the tooth fell out. He gripped it in his hand and ran toward his mother. She took the tooth, which was so tiny and white in the palm of her brown hand, and said, laughing, that it was the prettiest tooth she had ever seen. She took him in her arms and told him to wait, sitting on the wooden stool at the base of the fountain. It was the first day of summer. Because of the pain, he was the first to stand up; his mother was making coffee. She put a low table in front of him. She made him drink the sweetened milk and then eat the fresh fig. At the bottom of the glass was a gold coin. He looked at it attentively for a long time before handing it to his mother, who hid it for him with his first tooth in the secret place with her jewels. He

[45]

would throw the other teeth into the sea, casting them toward the sun, and standing at the edge of the surf he would say, like the other children he had already heard speak these words—I am throwing away a donkey's tooth, give me a gazelle's—repeating this phrase until he was no longer a child. Today his teeth are yellow with tobacco stains, like those of a horse, but strong. He found the other gold coin, the one his mother keeps with the first, at the bottom of his glass of sweetened milk just as the cannon boomed. It was his first day of fasting for Ramadhan, and he was probably seven years old. An entire day of fasting. At the sound of the cannon, he jumped toward his mother, who had already prepared a glass of milk with the gold coin in it just for him. It was on the low table, and next to it was a big soup bowl full of *chorba*, and he smelled the coriander as he drank the honey-sweetened milk. The gold coin was not any bigger than the one he received for his first tooth. His mother put it in a little purse attached to the belt of her dress.

8

The men are no longer playing dominoes. They are drinking beer and smoking. One of them talks quietly about his oldest son in the language of his brothers. He had a celebration for his oldest son far away from the old country. In the housing project, the brand new buildings built on the cleared hills a few miles from the city are not very tall. The women took care of the sheep. He bought two lambs from a farmer he knows. He fed them for a month before slaughtering them. The apartment buildings are separated from one another by a tract of rocky earth where no trees grow, but the men were able to construct a pen for the sheep, a separate space fenced in by wooden boards where the blood flows when the animals are killed. He invited the whole neighborhood. Nobody objected when the sheep were killed because he did it neatly, and the women waiting outside on the hill cleaned them and cut the meat up without making much noise. The girls in the families that fed the sheep had decorated them with henna, flowers, and colored ribbons. On the day of the sacrifice, they began to cry and didn't want to be present at the sacrifice. The oldest son was honored and spoiled by his mother and grandmother. He even had the right to the famous gold coins his mother was saving for him. But she returned to her house, saying she was too old to stay with her son and his family; she didn't want to die on foreign soil. After her departure, nothing happened the way it should have in their home in the housing project. He can't figure out why, but everything went wrong. His mother was no longer there to make sure the rules were respected. Perhaps his wife was too young; she tried to live like the other women, those who come from here, and he worked so hard he wasn't at home enough to know that. He thought that his wife along with the other women in the project would act like his mother, but nothing happened according to their traditions. He gave his wife money for the house and the children, but not all of his pay. He sent money orders, at first quite regularly, to his mother and later on to his sisters when they became pensionless widows. But the money he earned under the table he kept for himself. On Sundays, after the morning TV program, he would slip out without saying where he was going. He always played the horses. He would return at night, after sunset, walking home slowly. He would often win small sums. That Sunday, he won enough to buy a new engine for the family Peugeot. It's a long journey; his mother lives in the house he had built in the village, near the border. The streets are usually empty. On that day, about a hundred yards in front of the apartment buildings, which face each other, he sees a group of men and boys; there aren't any women or girls among them. The group is silent. He quickens his pace. He puts his hand to his breast pocket, where he has the pari-mutuel check. He can feel his heart beating

[47]

faster. No . . . why him? Why his family? His oldest son came back from a training session a week ago and is looking for work, but summer, particularly early summer, is a bad time to be looking for a job. He was offered one as a temporary farm laborer and hasn't turned it down yet, but he told his dad he prefers to stay here for the vacation. He'll see about work later.

The group of men and boys forms a semicircle, their eyes riveted on the sidewalk. He doesn't understand what is happening. He approaches and sees stones on the pavement. He keeps repeating to himself—Why my son, why my family—up to the moment he sees the stones on the ground in the form of a body—Why my son . . . Why my son . . . Why him . . . Why my son . . . He staggers toward the drawing traced in uneven stones that narrows at the spot where the head is drawn, widening at the bottom. He steps forward; the men watching him in silence move away—So it's my son. He fell at this spot, killed at the curb—but he can't see his son. With his jacket sleeve, he wipes away the beads of sweat on his forehead. He sees only a stain of dark blood that looks like black tar on the gray asphalt. The blood is in the shape of a man's body lying down; the children have placed stones from the hill around the pool of blood. Like the others, pressed against them, he too stares at the dark bloodstain encircled in white stones—Who says it's my son? Why my son? The men are silent. They live in the project; they know. They saw him collapse, bleeding, after the gunshots rang out. The women came running over before the police arrived. And despite the warnings— no one is allowed to touch a dead body lying in a public street—they picked up the young man's body, carrying it in their arms up to his mother's apartment. They stretched him out on the sofa; he wasn't bleeding anymore. His mother kneeled down next to him, took his hand, and whispered in his ear the prayer for the dead, swaying back and forth like a crazy old woman. The women sat around the sofa, huddled against the mother, who then covered her son's body with a sheet embroidered with gold arabesques. His head was resting on a cushion embroidered with the same arabesques. His wounds weren't visible. He'd been shot in the heart from behind. The women didn't make the little girls leave. They crouched down, clinging to their mothers and older sisters. When the women heard the police sirens, they encircled the body, covering it so the police wouldn't see it, and began to scream in unison, crying out against the violent, unjust death, a shriek of revolt against the rule that strangers must take a son's body away from his mother. She had given birth to him, and she has to protect him in death. Her son belongs to her, to her alone. The doorbell rings, but they refuse to open the door. Then the knocking grows louder. The women don't budge. Voices shout—police. The women are silent, motionless next to the sofa. They hear the sound of a key in the lock, and the door opens. The boy's father precedes the police, who wait in the hallway. The father enters the room, where the women have stopped weeping. He speaks to his wife; she says—I don't want to . . . I don't want to . . . I know what they are going to do to him . . . He's my son . . . He's mine. They killed him, and they are taking him away, they are stealing him from me. They can't rob a mother of her son. I don't want them to touch him. They're impious. If they take him, I go with them . . . He's my son; they don't have any right . . . I'll stay with him wherever they put him, even in the morgue . . . A mother stays with her son until he's put in the ground . . . The mother gets up, screams, grows agitated; she keeps the police away from the sofa. The chief gives an order, and the officers slide the stretcher under the boy's body. The mother screams; the father tries to calm her down. The women take her into the adjoining room, where she collapses in tears on the rug next to the bed. The stone tracing around the dried blood remained there for several days. Men and boys kept watch, then everyone in the housing project took away a pebble, and their brothers working for the street-cleaning service washed the stain away. The street-cleaning truck passed at dawn. The body was placed in a sealed coffin; after the investigation, the Amicale (Friends Society) helped with the expense of repatriating the body. The family left by plane, using the money won at the races.

The men in the café, sitting by the windows facing the sea, drink on into the night. They have stopped playing dominoes. They speak a language the women who were there in the afternoon don't understand. The women had been speaking among themselves, not listening to the men. They left the café quite a while ago, paying no attention to the foreign language. The man who lost at dominoes said his death will cost no one anything. He has never spoken to his wife about it; she never asks him anything. Even when he doesn't come home for two or three days, she never says anything. They speak very little to each other, if at all.

9

The gold coins hidden in the big house will disappear when the house collapses, just as his mother predicted, and either his maternal grandmother or his mother will give them to the oldest grandchild. She may already have done so when his younger brother had a son before coming here for the job that cost him his life. He knew his brother, a roofer, was killed when he fell from a roof he was tiling. The house back home needed him; he would have known how to repair it, and then he died abroad like a pariah. His brother said he liked working close to the sky. Sometimes, if there was a very high tree near the roof, he would climb down by going from branch to branch. His brother's wife, the little cousin with the curly blond hair, waited for him for years. He didn't want her and the children to join him. He planned to earn money to surprise her with a new house that he would build himself. But the sisters knocked on the green door. They were the first to know, because of the smoke coming from across the sea. The women of the big house were not ill, nor were the children. One was mentally retarded but physically sound. The women could tell by his mother's expression, her fear at the sight of the three old women, that one of the absent men would be coming back to be put in the ground. The sisters didn't stay. His mother would have chased them away herself, since there was no man to do so, and the son who had promised to return was perhaps dead and without a tomb in some foreign land. The women left the ruins, and the children warned their grandmother of the witches' nocturnal departure. She thought they would come back again to the courtyard with the dry fountain on the day of her own death. She thought too that she would know if something happened to her son. He must be alive and doesn't want to return.

10

In the white room on the other shore, the man is dying.

III

At the bend in the river, he fell.

Who will speak my mother's words to me? Who will be able to recite the prayer for the dead to me in the white room where I have been left alone? I can see no one, and no one hears me when I call from the other shore.

I

The man drank a lot of beer that Sunday, the first day of summer, in the café by the sea. He is speaking too loudly, and, laughing, he tells his startled domino companions that his death doesn't worry him; he isn't afraid. If he has a soul, and he is not really sure that he does, although he thinks he probably does, but sometimes it seems as if the devil is hiding under his black nails. He looks at his nails, the others do too, noting they aren't clipped short to keep away the devil. His mother and his maternal grandmother were right. Why is it that women are always right in the end . . .

If he has a soul, his body can be tossed into the public trash dump.

He has the café owner's promise that if he dies in the café, he will cast his body out to sea. That's what he would prefer, but who keeps a promise? Hadn't he himself promised his mother he would protect her from the three sisters? Who will do it if he isn't there at the right moment? He cleans his nails with a pocket knife. He tries to cut them, but the blade is dull; his fishing knife is old. The devil is keeping him here. Why? What's he doing here, anyway? His wife waited for him the first few years. His wife's house is not his home nor his children's. He has no children. If she had followed him to the big house out of a sense of love, for love alone, not reason, she would have had her own room, the courtyard with the clear fountain, the fig tree, the terrace where the women and girls chat. He would have taken care of the house and its pillars. He wouldn't have destroyed the swallow's nest, the ceilings, the edges of the inner balconies, and the green door. His mother would have welcomed his wife, the woman he married, bearing no mistrust. A foreigner is not a pariah. As for her words, her gestures, other women can recognize them as if they were their own. Tears and laughter are the same everywhere, and the body of a woman who has borne children in her house is like those of the women in the big house. Isn't that true? If a foreign woman has a child with the oldest son of the family, that child belongs to the grandmother's house, and the stranger, the mother of her son's son, is a member of the family. And if she isn't afraid of going to the public bath with the women of the big house, if she doesn't behave like a barbarian who wants to bathe privately, and if the others . . . If she doesn't hide her body when she's in the midst of the nude women washing together, if she allows the old women of the bath to lather and scrub her, remove her body hair, and perfume her with the fragrances the women adore, well, then, she won't be considered a foreigner. But all that can't happen in a day. His mother knows the foreigner will fit in after the birth of their first son. She will be vigilant and, if necessary, reprimand some of her daughters-in-law. The gold coins will be given to her son's oldest son. The foreigner listens to the women at the bath. She can't understand everything. Sometimes when someone speaks, languages blend. She follows the story of the three sisters. Will she see them one day? Every time she walks by the sea she is told not to go into the ancient city. The children have deserted it. The old women sleep and keep watch at the foot of the sanctuary. Nobody is able to describe their faces, but they claim to know about their lives before they began wandering. How can that be? What proof is there? The women who tell these tales don't need any proof. What they say is true since nobody doubts their words. Who doesn't respect the wisdom and piety of the old women of the bathhouse? They know what they are saying. They have been washing the bodies of young virgins for decades. The sisters have been washing the bodies of the dead for centuries, from sister to sister. People say the youngest was a shepherdess. She tended the village flocks on the arid plateaus with her young brothers. She never feared the wolves and protected her flocks against wild animals. It seems she knew how to speak to them, and in truth not a single animal of hers perished, was neither slaughtered nor carried away, whereas on the neighboring plateaus the peasants lamented their losses day after day. She had a gift, that's for sure. Her father refused to believe in his daughter's talents. As soon as she reached puberty, he took her away from the plateaus, and the wolves, and the flocks, which were decimated shortly thereafter, and he married her off to a rich miserly grocer who had just repudiated his third wife. The grocer shut his young wife away in a beautiful but sorrowful house and forbade her to speak with the old servant. She had one son before her husband married a younger wife who came to live in the same house and then another who bore him nine children. Each time he married, he favored the youngest wife and her children. He ne-

[55]

glected his oldest son, the child of the shepherdess who no longer spoke with the wolves and spent years sequestered in the grocer's house with the co-wives, who didn't like her. One day, her son disappeared, and she learned from a traveling salesman who had known her since childhood that he had joined the army of the nation occupying their land. At this point in the story, a woman contradicted the old woman, for she knew he had joined an elite fighting corps of one of the powerful tribes of the far south that was fighting the advancing enemy troops. She added that they were members of a famous brotherhood whose leader was also the tribal chief. The old woman of the baths affirmed that the mother believed the traveling salesman's story. Her son had indeed gone off to become a soldier and was reportedly killed by his kinsmen. People say that the night after she learned the news, she howled like a wolf and was seen the next morning before sunrise leaving the grocer's house in search of her son. Distraught, her hair unkempt, her dress unbelted, she left, taking nothing with her. Some women accompanied her to the end of the road leading to the plateaus, giving her enough provisions for several days and tidying her beautiful curly hair, which they covered with three headscarves. They fastened her dress with a woven wool belt and wrapped her in a veil that would protect her until she reached the next marabout's tomb. They received news of her from the traveling salesman. He had recognized her, a vagabond in rags praying at the foot of an isolated sanctuary, asking God to return her only son to her. The salesman claims she never knew her son died in a battle between the occupying army and the warriors of a tribe from the far south, and she didn't know he was buried with other foreign soldiers in a military cemetery far from the high plateau at the foot of a hastily constructed fortification topped with watchtowers. As she was passing by, it didn't occur to her to go up to the graves because of the crosses, and even if she had noticed that several graves were not marked by crosses, she wouldn't have been able to read the name of the soldier either in her own language or the language of the invader. Finally, she joined her sisters, the washers of the dead, probably thinking that in one of the houses she would recognize her son's body—by chance, and by breaking a rule—because women don't wash men's bodies, but she would know it was her son who was laid out in the room where he'd been washed. She would even risk her life to see him and steal him away from the family that had adopted him. The sisters would have taken him, knowing better than any strangers what should be done for an only son. Her sisters, the washers of the dead, would have approved of her gestures. Weak at first, they, like her, would have become strong enough to carry the cherished body to a river and place it beside the clear water on a long flat stone. These women are old; who would want to look at them, love them, caress them, impregnate them? Their bodies already belong to another world. They offend neither man nor God. They are so old, they are barely alive, mere memories of women. They wash their sister's son, still a strong young man who could have been a strong fearsome warrior able to face lions and tigers in order to protect the tribe, a man who would never have abandoned his mother, who is now destined to live a solitary life, begging and wandering. He fled, and his mother didn't curse him. On this flat stone, she blesses him like a child, cleansing him in water drawn from the river, purifying him in order to return him to God as pure as he was when she gave birth to him. The sisters accompany her gestures with kindly words. The youngest of them sings funeral chants that are more beautiful than any wedding songs. Wild horses come to drink at a bend in the river. Neighing and galloping on the plain, they approach the women bending over the son. If wolves ran to the riverbank, the youngest would speak to them, and they would move away from the stone. The women tell each other, whispering, that this man, their sister's son, is handsome. The youngest knows how handsome a man can be, but the others don't, for a man as handsome as the one they are perfuming with wild grasses has never leaned toward either one of them on the high bed in the bedroom. They were young once, and like the other girls and women, they too dreamed about the most handsome daring man who would take them away from the guarded walls. No man came for them, except the one they did not love but endured night after night in violence and distress until they fled. And they touch this man lying gently at the riverbank, they touch his body as if they had never touched a man's body before; they are young women in love once more and ready to embrace the man who might have loved them. Using miraculous plants they alone know will restore their sister's son to life, they take turns rubbing him, warming his face, his chest just above his heart; they work passionately until they feel the breath of life, first as a child's breath and then as a man's, not the breath of a soldier who drank too much alcohol in cabarets filled with misery. The sisters make a fire near the stone. They rub his body for hours on end until the first jackal howls in the night. In spite of the fire, the body grows cold again. They despair. Who but God has the right to bring the dead back to life? They resign themselves, looking one more time at the body that has grown stiff. His mother wraps him in the veil she has kept since the day she fled to the plateaus. This will be his shroud. She ties it with a willow branch at his head and feet. The sisters guard the man's body, the most handsome of all men, the last one they are allowed to see, to touch, and to love. At dawn, they climb up toward the marabout's tomb at the crest of the hill. To dig the grave, they use neither bits of wood nor jagged pebbles but work with their hands, bent over. Exhausted at the end of the day, at sunset, they cover the grave with the flat stones pious women place against the sanctuary walls. They collect dry brambles with long deadly thorns to protect the tomb from nocturnal animals.

[58]

They cover it with these thorny plants, and then the oldest, most dexterous one who taught her sons how to carve bows and arrows sculpts arabesques on two olive branches, one for the head, one for the feet, signs that no one will touch; the tallest is for the head. They don't need to tell the women guarding the sanctuary to watch over their son's tomb. These poor old women, filled with piety, have shared with them their dry wheat cakes, the olive branch placed on the grave, and the dried figs they keep in reserve for vagabonds and pilgrims who have lost their way.

2

But his wife said no. She refused to cross the sea to live in the big house he would have repaired, because at that time he loved her. She said no every time he spoke of the village, of his mother, the ruins, the port where he fished as a child, the open sea, the rough waves that more than once almost capsized the heavy boat the old fisherman who sat on the terrace of his house by the port would lend to spunky children who would return with the largest and rarest fish. And then she no longer said no because he wasn't there to hear her. He would come back to his wife's house as long as he knew she was expecting him. He came back for her, the woman who always refused the journey but not the child they could never have, nor him. Now when he returns, she is no longer waiting for him. She is there, at home. He leaves but doesn't cross the sea. His ear isn't ringing yet; the leaf from the tree of life, his mother's leaf, has not yet brushed against his own as it falls—he will begin his final journey the day it does. While he waits, he spends his time in the seaside café. It's almost night, and he talks, smokes, drinks. He writes letters for his companions in exile. He asks them to remind him of the prayer that must be recited when one's ear rings for a long time, even longer for a mother. One man says that whatever leaf falls, the prayer is the same. He lowers his voice to recite it above the sound of the scattered dominoes, surrounded by the smell of beer and cheap tobacco. They roll their cigarettes with gray tobacco, but he smokes corn-paper Gitanes. The café proprietor says he's going to close. They are the last ones there. They ask for a drink, and the proprietor grumbles, says that after this one he's closing. Slowly, they pack up their dominoes. The man smoking Gitanes pulls out a wad of papers from his breast pocket. He writes when he is alone and doesn't want to go home to his wife. No one but these companions, city nomads like himself whom he meets just once, know he writes. Sometimes he leaves them without even asking their names, and if they're not asked, or if he doesn't say his name first, they don't give theirs. Perhaps he drank too much that time, because it took some time for him to recall his name. That worried him; it has happened three times. Today, in the seaside café that is about to close, he says his name without hesitating to the domino companions he will leave after the last beer. They too say their names. They say good-bye to each other in their native language, according to their custom. He spreads the sheets of paper on the table, setting them out like playing cards. Then, putting them in a row for a game of solitaire, he reads the numbers out of order, mixes them up, and gives out pages indiscriminately to each of his companions, who glance at the pages without reading them. He writes when he feels the urge, sometimes in verse, sometimes not, disjointed stories he alone can understand. From time to time, he reads his work aloud to men who are like him and who listen to him. If his mother knew how to read . . . he would have sent her all the pages he ripped up. Then she would know her son is a poet. He said nothing to his wife. The first few years, he wrote poems for her and gave her some. She must have read them. Did she save them? She never spoke to him about them; it was as if he had never written them. For a long time now he has been writing and never tells anyone he might see again.

One night, he came back home to his wife's house, this time having written a story, and not thinking to hide the sheets of paper as he usually did. He even continued writing at the kitchen table and must have fallen asleep. He doesn't know how he did it, but he left everything scattered on the table and the floor. When he woke up, he was alone in bed—he no longer slept in the same bed as his wife—he got up, his coffee was ready in the kitchen. He found nothing there, not one sheet of paper. He looked everywhere, in the drawers, the closets, on the night tables, on the shelves, under the stacks of linen, behind the furniture, in the garbage cans, and found nothing. He drank his coffee before searching once again. In the summer, his wife lowers the fireplace screen. In old buildings, there are fireplaces that work. His wife had wanted an apartment with a fireplace, like the one in her mother's house in the country. He found her one. After drinking his last cup of coffee, he thought of the fireplace. He raised the fire screen. Tiny charred papers blew out. He wondered for a moment if he hadn't imagined these pages, the countless days spent in the city, the nights. He forgot what he had written. Neither he nor his wife said a word. He collects the sheets of paper and begins to read. The café owner shuts the cash register without listening to him, says he's closing. The men leave the seaside café. The café owner says—See you later, it is already morning—and pulls down the iron shutter from inside the café.

The man is alone. He goes toward the sea, his shoes in his hand. He walks in the foam; it is not yet daybreak. He reaches the spot where the river meets the sea. Next time he won't forget to tell the café owner that if he drops dead at the foot of the counter, as predicted, his body should be cast out to sea, just where the river and sea come together; that is what he wants done. Perhaps the café owner will have trouble getting his body through the sand up to that point. There's no road, and you have to go along the edge of the waves; the sand is harder there, and it is possible to push a wagon. He has seen an old wagon in the shed behind the café. If the proprietor hesitates— for the moment he has agreed, thinking he won't have to do it because the man frequents other bistros besides his—he will give him some money in advance. If he turns around, on the left, he can see the closest ruins. First, the rosemary plants that grow between the stones in the hollow he knows so well, the beehives surrounded by thyme, and before you reach the first broken wall, the laurel bushes on each side of the river that cuts a channel in the sand as it flows out to sea. Beyond the ruins and the eucalyptus bordering the coast road, the first hills appear, and higher up, the hill of wheat, and the lone tree where men and beasts rest. His mother told him about the child killed by a blow from the horse's hoof. From his breast pocket he pulls out the packet of papers covered with writing, with thin, well-shaped letters on each page, no margins and not one blank space on either the sides, the top, or the bottom of the pages that only he can read. Who would make the effort to decipher such handwriting, the pages are so full, the text of an unknown man who writes poems and stories no one will read because he keeps his nocturnal inspiration a secret? He moistens the index finger of his right hand, takes the sheets of paper one by one, puts together the odd-numbered pages, places the even-numbered sheets in his jacket, and carefully rips the pages he has been keeping into pieces as light as confetti. Who could put back together even the smallest word? He holds the shredded pages in his hands, walks toward the spot where the merging waters form a whirlpool, and throws them away with the same expansive solemn gestures as the ancients who tossed the ashes of their loved ones on the banks of the sea surrounded by countries that have been at war for so long, and it isn't over yet. But war is also an encounter, and the whirlpool where the papers disappear marks the turbulent exchange between the river and the sea. Why does he suddenly think

[62]

of a picture he cut out and folded in his wallet? Why did he do it? He was leafing through a newspaper he found on a bistro table when this photo caught his eye: thirty or maybe fifty bodies laid out on stretchers on the ground, lined up in several rows, covered with military blankets knotted at the head and feet. A photo with no caption. He didn't read the article but tore out the page like a thief. He quickly folded it in eighths, and since then it has been in his wallet along with his papers. Are these bodies the price we pay for impossible crossings? Poems never read by other eyes, other voices? Who will know if they are beautiful? Endless bits of paper reduced to tiny ashes by the merging currents. The ash is as fine as the flour he secretly touched in the big house. Flour is never tossed in the sea . . . the first seed is buried in the ground. His mother told him never to lose it like some idiot. It is sacred. You will burn in hell forever if you throw the golden powder in the sea just for the fun of it. The sea is sterile and doesn't produce grain like the earth. You must give the sea no offering; she will take your life if you are an unlucky fisherman, abandoned by God. Abandoned by God, his mother will never know that he forgot God and that God abandoned him. Is that why he writes poems destined for oblivion? He recalls a man he once met in a public bathhouse. He was a pious talkative soul who had come back from the Holy Land. Why was he living in a foreign land at an age when misfortune could strike at any moment? He never explained. He glorified those who wanted to die on sacred land and said that he, sick and impotent, would return to the Holy Land to die. That's how one earns a place next to God. He explained that one day he had lost his papers and all his possessions. He had prayed all night, and in the morning he found his suitcase as well as his papers, billfold, and money; nothing was missing. Listening to this man, he couldn't understand the whims of old men who are frightened at the moment of death, who demand to be buried in sacred land, making their

[63]

children promise to sacrifice outlandish sums of money in order to carry out this last filial duty. But the garrulous old man affirmed that this death complied with religious requirements, and the other men agreed. What would he have said? Who would have listened to him? If he had said that poets, not all poets, but those who celebrate liberty, the only liberty there is—difficult to obtain, illusory, cruel—will sit closest to God, the men would have considered him impious because they think that poems must sing the praises of one God. If they don't, the poets and their poems are unworthy of the Almighty and should be burned. He left the public bath thinking about his wife's words.

She no longer spoke to him, and he didn't say much to her either, but her father had just died, and he didn't want to leave her alone. He didn't attend the funeral service, but he did go to the burial. On the tomb, his wife's paternal family vault, he read his wife's maiden name, her father's name. That very evening when they were watching television, she asked him if he ever thought about his own death. He burst out laughing—Why are you laughing?—Are you saying that because you want to see me dead? What would you want to do with me when I'm dead? What if I don't die in your house, what if I'm far away? You won't know where, even if I'm taken to a hospital, because I'll have been picked up on a public street, and I won't give my name. They won't be able to identify me, and you won't be notified. So, what do you propose for my death, you, my wife who didn't give me one bit of your life here? Tell me—In my father's burial plot, there are still two places, one for me, and one for you, if you wish—He burst out laughing again. Why are you laughing like that?—You're asking me? You and I united in death after all these years we each spent with our own unhappiness, incapable of moving on, clinging to one another. What kind of life is this? A disastrous fate, separate but stuck together, and you hope that in death . . . You refused to live in the big house across the sea, a woman among women, vibrant, joyous—my woman, my wife, the mother of my children, my lover, my sister . . . You refused all that, and you want to drag me with you into your father's vault in one of those city cemeteries when we could have been buried together in the maritime cemetery on the hill . . . No . . . What I'm saying isn't true. You were right not to try to live on the other shore, you were right . . . What would have happened? You would have been eaten alive by the women of the big house. They would have attacked you, because you are too fragile, too white, too blond, your eyes too blue. They would have torn you to pieces, those furies. I know them; I've seen them gang up against a woman from the capital. Those crazy dangerous women would have sent her off to an insane asylum if she hadn't left of her own accord, terrified for years afterward. And you . . . No, we would have had to take you away from the big house and the women. But where could we go? I wouldn't have been able to build a house for you on some other hill. You were right not to cross the sea. You would have come back to your father's house before it was time to think of any cemetery plot, more unhappy than ever. But don't wait for my death to shut me away with you in the tomb of a family that never liked me. Think about your death as much as you want and leave me mine so that I can offer my corpse to the jackals or the dogs. I don't want to be like those poor souls who fought the wrong war and were fooled for years. They were told they would have a house more beautiful than the ruined houses on the high plateaus and mountains. They would have privileges no one before them had received, and their wives, children, and grandchildren would be the happiest. And today, why is it that the mothers and daughters of these men have been so preoccupied, for such a long time now, with the tombs of their fathers, sons, and brothers? Why is it that these women who are so close to death, through birth and illness, know, like the women magicians, what is most important? How many times did the daughters of the betrayed men travel for miles on the roads of this country that didn't give the men decent housing, so that the foreign land wouldn't remain a hostile one, and not forget them? The girls and sisters crossed the country on foot to keep alive the memory of their fathers and brothers. Miserable remains that no one honors, flowers placed on their graves once a year recall their mistakes and the fact that they died as orphans in shame. The daughters love their ostracized fathers, the sisters their disinherited brothers. These women alone have prayers said in the part of the cemetery granted to the pariahs by other men, their hands joined above the graves, palms turned to the sky, who recite the prayers for the dead. These brothers in misfortune fear being forgotten by their own families and hasten to accomplish the religious ritual that others will carry out for them if they have daughters and sisters who follow tradition, so that they won't be cursed at the time of death and afterward, cursed as they were when they were living. In the villages and small cities where he stopped, on the square facing the café where he goes alone or with others, there are monuments to the dead. He has never read the name of a soldier from overseas who died for this country. Only the names of native sons are inscribed, not those who came from afar, even if they fell at the very site where the monument was erected. What about his native village? He won't go back there to check whether or not the name of the dead is etched on monuments that no longer exist anywhere, if they ever did. His wife asks him why he is talking about that, what does it have to do with what she said. Nothing. He left in the morning. He hadn't spoken to his wife at length for a long time. Was he really talking to her? It had been years.

3

The man walks along the river toward the seaside café and stands there alone in the sea dawn. He doesn't feel like fishing. Will his poems in shreds in the merging waters reach the other shore intact? If the flocks of swallows snatch the poet's confetti, each bird carrying a piece in its beak without dropping it until the birds reach the edge of the ruins they know or the terrace of the big house, who will take the trouble to pick up the tiny scraps of paper and piece back together the poems he had tossed into the sea? If the swallows who aren't afraid of the sisters place their booty at the foot of the sanctuary the sisters occupy, what will they do with the fragile pieces? The youngest sister, the only literate one, deciphered the message brought by the swallows; poems from beyond the tomb. The woman sits down and pieces together the scattered pieces of paper brought to the ruins by the swallows. She assembles them on her prayer rug, studies them, tries to read the almost illegible letters. By what magic did each poem find its proper place several days later? She reads aloud to her sisters, who don't understand these poems carried to them on the winds. One night, the youngest sister went up to the village alone. No one saw her slip under the green door (which has not been stripped or repainted as it should have been) the sheets of paper the son, with his fine illegible handwriting, wrote poems on. The man doesn't climb back toward the Roman ruins between the laurel bushes. He moves away from the swirling waters that would carry him off, if it were God's will. He walks along the river, no one walking in step with him on the opposite bank. He sees the lights of the cabaret at the water's edge, the one that closes at sunrise. In his pocket, next to the poems, he has a few remaining bills; he hasn't lost all his cash playing dominoes. He checks; he'll be chased away like a beggar if he goes in there without any money. He hears the shrill nasal music of the musical groups that come through the village as they head for the hills, playing their flutes and drums from the far south. The black men dressed like warrior musicians scare him a bit. The first time he saw them, he was probably three years old. He stayed close to his mother, who was huddled next to the other women of the house at the threshold of the door that opened onto the tall Africans dancing in the middle of the street. The cabaret musicians aren't black. They are three brown-skinned men who have been there ever since he began coming to the riverside cabaret. The women change, but not the one who works the cash register. He has never seen her standing. He notices her filmy gauze dresses with short sleeves, a bit tight at the arms, and her gold jewelry. Her heavy white neck is partly hidden by her necklaces. She likes pink, green, and mauve. Her hair is black, curled on her forehead. The cabaret owner is talkative. That's how he learned about Soraya, the fortune-teller who disappeared, although he is sure she will warn him at the appropriate moment. She promised she would do so wherever she happened to be, and he believes her. He learned from the cabaret owner that Soraya spent several months with her. She wanted to keep her; the men liked her, and she liked her voice, but she didn't stay. What has become of her? She thinks she will return. She only learned a few weeks ago that Soraya was born in the same region as she was. They talked together about the sisters. The man listens, saying nothing about his own native village. The woman cabaret owner often speaks to him because he doesn't interrupt her like the others.

She says that she doesn't believe in the sisters' magic powers. They are poor old penniless women who wash the dead because in the houses where they offer their services no one else wants to do it; they are fed there. The women are victims of misfortune. Why are they called sisters? No one knows anything about them. People say that the oldest, the one who limps and walks with a cane, had seven sons and seven daughters—a happy fulfilled mother whom the other women, particularly the sterile wives, were jealous of. She lived with her children and her servants in a house as big as a palace. The boys and girls played in the gardens, the orchards, the large mosaic fountains. They raised animals and rare birds, gazelles, peacocks, and doves. The boys took care of the horses and the falcons. They had teachers who taught them at home like princes. Why did misfortune strike her family this way? No one knows why. Did jealous women finally succeed in causing her harm with their spells? They and others tried to destroy this chosen family's happiness. The seven sons and seven daughters died, buried by an earthquake that went on for several days. Only the mother was spared, but she had nothing left. The villagers were relocated. A room was reserved for her, but she never occupied it. No one in the little town knew what became of her. Only much later did they think they recognized her as the washer of the dead who replaced the last village woman who had done it before her. The sisters who are not really sisters are poor harmless women, slightly crazy. They are neither magicians nor priestesses, nor witches of any kind, but vagabonds who do honorable but degrading work. That's what the fearful living think about them. The woman cabaret owner says vehemently that she isn't afraid of them, and if they were to come knocking at her door—and why wouldn't that happen, for they appear everywhere, not only in the ruins of the ancient city—she would open the door herself, recognizing the oldest sister's cane. She would offer them hospitality and have her black servant, the one who came here with her and has never left, bring out fruit and cakes, bowls of warm water for each one of them, white towels, and the prettiest house slippers. She would wash their feet, one after the other, not giving the task to anyone else, not even to her faithful sweet Negress. In spite of what the black servant says, these women are not evil. She will pay for their pilgrimage to the holy sites. In fact, several years from now, she herself will sell the business, and before growing old in the village where she is having her house built on the cool hills above the ruins, she will make the pilgrimage. In her town flows a tributary of the river she got permission to divert. Friends in high places come to spend a few days at her place; they are fed, lodged, and pampered. One night the daughter of one of them knocked at her door. She didn't recognize her. She learned she had been in prison, didn't know where to go, had no money, no friends. She didn't give her work; she didn't want to hire a mixed-up girl. One morning, her servant found a syringe under the bed while cleaning the room. That very evening, she admitted everything, her running away, the drugs, illness, prison, the fact that her boyfriend's parents intervened to put her in prison, the baby she didn't have because it died in the womb, and then she needed an emergency operation, and now this deadly illness. She didn't chase the girl away, but the girl disappeared one night, taking with her everything she could find, her money, jewels—luckily the rest is kept in the bank—and she didn't rob the clients. The girl's father is looking for her. He will never find her. He doesn't know she'll be dead in a few months. They told her that in prison. When she was released, they gave her the address of a hospice, and then she came to the cabaret. If the sisters had been there, they would have taken care of her in her last days, treating her with tenderness, she's sure of that. The girl's body wouldn't have stayed in the morgue, waiting in vain for someone to claim it, and she wouldn't have been hastily buried in a corner of the cemetery reserved for the paupers, with no mourners and only her name and young age recorded. The cabaret owner tells the man this story is true; she doesn't know if the girl is still alive or not, but she has no doubts about her misfortune or her death as a vagabond. She has seen other young women come through and has given them work; she always did what she could. Their lives on both shores were tragic. How many has she taken in since becoming the owner of the cabaret at the river's edge, as if the current helped them find their way to her door? If the women who work for her, dancing and singing for men, are in trouble, the men sense it and don't like it. They want happy musicians, graceful young dancers, women who know how to talk and entertain. How can they desire and be seduced by them if the women don't believe in happiness? She has saved more than one but couldn't prevent the suicide of one young girl who was as lost as the others who no longer wished to live. She thought she would have to close the cabaret then, but her clients testified to her good intentions. The young girl threw herself from the balcony window facing the river, and the current carried her away. The body was found and had to be identified. The girl was wearing a transparent summer gown covered with sequins; her hair was still tied with a long ribbon embroidered with gold thread that a client had given her. She took charge of sending the coffin to the family. She took care of everything, explaining that the girl had been killed in a traffic accident; the authorities didn't attempt to contradict her. From that day on she has hired only professionals. The clients prefer it that way.

The man sits on a red cushion covering the stone sofa in front of a little carved wooden table. He is smoking and drinking. A woman is singing; he isn't looking at her. She's a young girl. She's singing a long way from the sofa; she's singing a song of love and death in his mother tongue. A frail silhouette in a pale green dress as light as foam. She wears no jewels; they would shine in the electric light that forms a white circle on the little wooden platform. Her hair is blond and curly, held in place by a straight hair band. He's attentive to her voice but doesn't look at her. He won't talk to the cabaret owner about the favor he asked of the owner of the seaside café. She wouldn't easily agree to put him in the water flowing beneath the windows of the lighted house where a very young girl is singing; he would have to live here to hear her sing; she alone; he must make her stay. He would pay whatever he has to pay to have her sing as he lies dying; she mustn't stop immediately. He wants to hear her before his body grows cold and stiff. Afterward . . . It doesn't matter. The men listen to her, mesmerized. She isn't as beautiful as the sexy dancers with soft round bellies as white as a dove's feather, and so agile. The men say nothing. When a woman dances they urge her on with their voices and clap their hands. She goes toward them to get the coins and bills they stick on her forehead and in her low-cut blouse. The singer doesn't move. She sings, standing tall on the small stage. The windows facing the river are open. It's summer. The weather is cool before daybreak. The men are standing around her; he approaches, looks at the young girl, whose eyes stare off toward the river as if the men were not there so close to her. Suddenly, the man shudders, draws back, and staggers to the red cushions on the sofa. He wasn't in the big house when she was born and didn't get the news because he hadn't sent them his address the first few years. He learned by chance that his younger brother had had a daughter before coming here to work and then die between the land and the sky. He recognized his little cousin's daughter, his brother's daughter. Her hair, like her mother's hair, which she hid under headscarves pulled tight at her temples and on her forehead. The daughter doesn't believe, as her mother did, that curly hair isn't pretty. He sees her face between two clients' shoulders. She is still singing. May she sing until daybreak and leave the cabaret as soon as she has finished, so he won't have the time to tell her who he is. One of the men goes toward her and places a gold sequin on her forehead covered with beads of sweat, and then two, then three more do the same. The young girl, confused, stops singing, takes the gold coins in her hand. Why did she stop singing? She smiles, shakes her curly hair, wipes the sweat off her brow. Her hair is golden, like her voice. The man closes his eyes, leans against the stone. She sings again. He was afraid he would no longer hear her or see her among the men. She is standing on the stage, luminous. He begins to write very quickly on a carved wooden table. No one notices him. The proprietor has left the cash register. She is standing at the edge of the stage, imposing in her filmy pink dress ruffled under her bosom, wide around her thin ankles. She is wearing house slippers the color of her dress, decorated with pearls and swan feathers. One lone flute accompanies the song. The man sitting on the sofa writes, not lifting his eyes toward the group of people clustered around the halo of light. He doesn't know if the gold sequins are sequins or gold coins like the ones his mother hid among her jewelry for the first son or daughter of her oldest son. Soon the sun will rise. And how can he live without the voice of the big house, for he hears a voice from his childhood, from the hills and the sea. He wants to return with this voice accompanying him, even though women aren't supposed to follow the funeral procession or enter the cemetery at the same time as the men and those who recite prayers. He doesn't want the clear tender voice to leave him; he doesn't want the girl who is singing to cover the hair curling at her forehead, her temples, and her neck when she puts it in a chignon. He wants to hear that voice in the grave, and before being buried in the depths of the earth, he wants to see a woman, a young girl singing, her face moistened with sea mist in the maritime cemetery where she stands against the wall of the white-domed sanctuary, where his mother has been asking to be buried for years, after her granddaughter, in a state of purity, has watched over her, perfumed her body, and enclosed her in the shroud she alone has the right to touch; and she will protect her from the three sisters, since her son, the one walking by the river, hasn't kept his promise. Did the young girl who is singing obey the old woman and stay alone with her for three days and three nights in the room that opens on the fountain, protecting her from the three sisters, all three standing behind the green door? Perhaps her song made the fountain flow for three days and three nights. The man sitting on the sofa writes; the others turn their backs to him. The sun is going to rise, and so he hurries. He writes as long as the young girl sings. With

[73]

the sheets of paper in his hand, he rises, goes down to the basement, enters the Turkish toilets, and stumbles against the water bottle. He rips the poems into small even squares, which he carefully throws down the hole, every one of them. The toilet flush is noisy, but it works. He watches the pieces of paper spread out on both sides of the ceramic tile feet with their checkerboard design and then disappear into the hole, propelled by the stream of water. He flushes three times. The porcelain is white and clean. The large room of the cabaret is empty when he comes back upstairs. The proprietor says she's going to close; she's tired. She has no room for her client, having given the room that used to belong to the girl who doesn't come to see her anymore to the young singer she wants to protect from the cabaret crowd, otherwise one of them, the wealthiest, will keep her for himself if he marries her, or he will make her work under his super-vision. She won't be able to resist. Who has taught her how to defend herself in a place where girls like herself know nothing of life? She never asked her anything, why she was there, where she had come from, who her father was. She heard her sing at a wedding once, for a family that does business in both countries. She was given hospitality in exchange for her singing; she invited her home. Before her pil-grimage, she will find the girl a perfect husband, something she hasn't found for herself, but then she can't sing that well. She will be the best singer and will travel throughout the world like the women we see on TV. She will be invited to shows where famous singers are seen and heard, like those black women from America. One night, her servant called her persistently to come and see this black singer speaking in a foreign language—her words were being translated as she spoke. She was an impressive woman, tall and strong like me, dressed in a shiny formal evening gown; she was magnificent. She sang, standing in front of the microphone. She was in clear view. They shut off the TV after she left the stage. So, why not my dove? I'll feed her well; she's a little thin. I'll hire a voice teacher for her. I prefer a woman; I'll get the best. I'll be able to do that. I'll find a husband for her later. If I do everything for her, she won't betray me. We will see her on the most famous stages, all over the world, and I'll be able to go, in peace, to the holy places and back to my native village. She'll come to see me there. She'll sing for all of us, a grand performance in the theater in the ancient ruins. I want to be there when she triumphs back home and know before I die that her voice is being heard beyond the sea and the mountains and in the maritime cemetery where I'll be keeping watch; her voice will reach to the depths of the earth.

4

The man listens to the excited cabaret owner. He doesn't think she is hallucinating. He believes what she says and that this tale is no lie. He will be there tonight and the next nights accompanied by the women and children of the big house. The men will be back; they too are drawn to the voice and the amazing young song, the song of the ancestors from the village and the lands across the sea. Each one will think that death may seize him at that very moment, and the sisters standing next to the cypress trees in the Roman sanctuary will be listening to the young girl singing. The children won't run away. The women won't hide their faces. The men will be silent as they stroke the hair of the little children leaning against their legs. His mother will no longer be hostile to the three sisters. The cabaret proprietor smiles. The sun is rising over the river; a bee flies above the flowering rosemary bush at the edge of the open window facing the water. The man goes toward the door; the woman accompanies him, a sudden breeze puffing out her filmy pink dress, although the river is so calm. The man suddenly stops as he opens the door. The woman standing near him utters a faint cry. The three sisters have stopped on the threshold. They have come in search of the young girl, the little cousin's daughter; her mother is calling for her. They have traveled the length and breadth of this foreign land. They know she is in the house by the river and is still asleep. They will wait; they have the time; they don't want to frighten her. The woman spreads out her arms, her body barring the entrance. The old women won't come into her house. She won't allow them to take the young girl away from her, not she who has shown the girl hospitality. Let them take her instead; her life is over . . . Why her protégée, who is so young? If necessary, she will take her young protégée to her mother's house; she will take charge of this. But the sisters must leave. The old women do not budge. The woman, her hands stretched out like a cross, forbids them to enter her house. The gauze of her dress billows, the breeze grows stronger, the window is darkened by a swarm of buzzing bees. The man lying on the ground, across the threshold, regains consciousness. A light pink fabric softly touches his face. The cabaret owner is kneeling beside him. He asks if the sisters have left, if they have taken away his brother's daughter. He wants to see her asleep before he leaves, to be sure she is resting in her bedroom, above the big room. The woman helps him to his feet. They go to the room. He can't see the young girl's face, only her hair falling in curls across the pillow embroidered with gold arabesques. He touches her hair lightly, turns toward the woman, who is yawning. She says she's going to sleep on the rug at the foot of the young girl's bed. He shouldn't worry. She will keep watch.

5

The man left the cabaret and walked along the riverbank one summer morning just after dawn. A man asked him for a light, speaking in his native tongue. He didn't hesitate. The man was a stranger. They remained silent for a long while and fell into step, walking side by side. The man began speaking, after they passed the bridge, as if he were speaking to himself. From time to time a swallow flew by at their feet to grab a white feather, a fine duvet left there by wild ducks the previous season. He talked about a childhood friend. They had gone to school together, and in the summer they watched their flocks in the mountains. They parted when the war broke out and met up again in the same resistance group. One of them almost died in the resistance, and the other spent time in prison, where his friend helped him until their country was liberated, but they didn't remain there. They didn't cross the sea in the same boat but ran into each other again in the other country. They have lived together as brothers for more than fifty years, and now his friend is going to leave him. He has learned he is in the hospital, dying. He didn't know he was so sick. He wasn't able to speak to him, and when he went to the hospital ward where he'd been brought in critical condition, he was no longer conscious. Would he regain consciousness? He thought he would because of the sun, and the clear sky, and because it was the first day of summer. He approached him; the nurse had just closed the door. He sat down close to him and, leaning toward his ear, recited the prayer for the dead in the language of the mountains, the gruff language of his childhood, far from the plains and the cities, mixing sacred words with those spoken by shepherds. His eyelids and lips trembled. He heard his voice whisper the friendly words he slipped in with the prayer. He died that evening on that summer day, and they hadn't told each other their last wishes. They hadn't thought about it, having escaped death so often . . . Several days later he was holding the censor filled with ashes. His friend's wife, who didn't speak their language, didn't want to keep the urn in her room. They spread the dead man's ashes in the garden out back on a patch of land. The ashes were spread lightly, powder sprinkled on this foreign soil. He didn't recite the prayer aloud as he swung the censor. He said the prayer for the dead several

[77]

times as if he were whispering it in his friend's ear. This happened three weeks ago. His wife returned to the country without him. His children live in foreign lands. He is alone. He wonders if the soul resists fire. The man smoking corn-paper Gitanes doesn't answer. His companion on the towpath continues his monologue; he has thought a lot about the ashes and the urn; it's lighter and less expensive than a leaded coffin, because he doesn't want a grave in one of the cemeteries here. He is going to write to his oldest son to explain this to him so that he can make his mother understand that it will be easier for her to get the urn. If she refuses on religious principles, the son should take charge of it; his son must obey him and bury the urn under the ancient olive tree, the ancestral tree, on the wheat hill. He must ask a pious man to watch over the funeral, making sure it goes according to the rules, and he must plant a solid olive-wood marker, one etched with his name, date of birth, and date of death. He is sure no one will desecrate his grave. He is going to write to his son tonight to tell him all this. He has made up his mind, and nothing will make him change it. And what about him? Has he thought about that day? The man doesn't answer; he quickens his pace. On his left, on the other side of this secondary road, a café has just opened. They say good-bye with a blessing and the ancient gesture of their right hand placed over their heart. The man crosses the road, enters the café; he doesn't look back.

6

The man continues his way along the river. He searches through his wallet and takes out the only identity card that has his name on it. He hasn't carried any other official papers for years. He takes off the photo and burns it on the iron grate, his cigarette lighter makes round marks at the foot of the lime tree; he buries the ashes in the ground, leans toward the river, and tosses away the card; his eyes follow it for a moment. When it has disappeared, he goes on his way once again.

A voice reaches him. Young, clear, and gilded like the sunlight on the river. He walks faster. The little cousin's daughter, his niece with the curly blond hair, the cabaret at the water's edge, the voice of the big house and the maritime cemetery.

He walks faster and faster.

7

The man hovers close to death on the foreign shore.

At the bend in the river, he falls.

In the white room, on the other shore, he is not alone. A man, sitting next to the dying man, whispers the prayer for the dead in his ear in his mother tongue. He repeats it three times.